S0-BUB-545

LIGHTHOUSE POINT

An Anthology of Santa Cruz Writers

LIGHTHOUSE POINT

An Anthology of Santa Cruz Writers

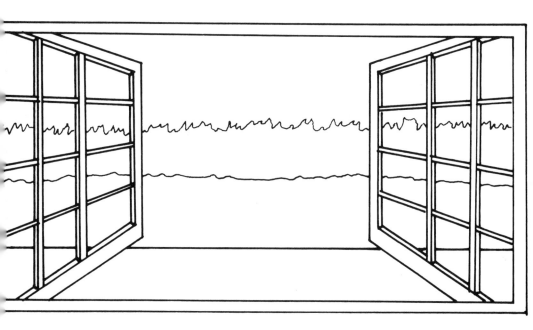

Edited by Patrice Vecchione and Steve Wiesinger

M PRESS
Soquel, California

M PRESS
4605 Fairway Drive
Soquel, California 95073

Cover art by Nathalie de la Rozière
Book design by Felicia Rice of Moving Parts Press, Santa Cruz
Typeset by TypaGraphix, Santa Cruz
Printed by BookCrafters, Chelsea, Michigan

Copyright © 1987 by Nathalie de la Rozière for M PRESS.
All rights revert to authors on publication.

ISBN 0-9619004-1-5

ACKNOWLEDGMENTS

"Plum" by Charles Atkinson appeared in *Poetry*, 7/84.

"In the Photograph" by Ellen Bass is reprinted from *Lesbian Words: A Santa Cruz Anthology*, copyright 1984 by Sue McCabe and Irene Reti, HerBooks.

"Renegade Christmas" by William Everson is reprinted from *Masks of Drought*, copyright 1980 by the author, Black Sparrow Press.

"Old Man Finds What Was Lost" by James B. Hall appeared in *New Letters*, 1984.

"The Dangerous Uncle" by James D. Houston is reprinted from *The Men in My Life*, copyright 1987 by the author, Creative Arts Books.

"The Blood Myth" by Robert Lundquist is reprinted from *before/THE RAIN*, copyright 1985 by the author, Moving Parts Press.

"How Does It Look to You" by Robert McDowell is reprinted from *Quiet Money*, copyright 1987 by the author, Henry Holt and Company.

"Song of the Andoumboulou: 13" by Nathaniel Mackey appeared in *Callalou VII*, 1985.

"In 1943, the Boy Imagines That" by Morton Marcus appeared in *Tri Quarterly #58*, 1983.

"I Think of Those Mornings" by Morton Marcus is reprinted from *Big Winds, Glass Mornings, Shadows Cast by Stars*, copyright 1981 by the author, Jazz Press.

"Corcoran Lagoon" by Maude Meehan is reprinted from *Chipping Bone*, copyright 1985 by the author, Embers Press.

"Dream-Vision" by Tillie Olsen is reprinted from *Mother to Daughter, Daughter to Mother*, copyright 1984 by the author, The Feminist Press.

"A Show of Strength" by Victor Perera is reprinted from *Rites: A Guatemalan Boyhood*, copyright 1986 by the author, Harcourt, Brace, Jovanovich.

"Baseball" by Robert Peterson is reprinted from *The Only Piano Player in La Paz*, copyright 1985 by the author, Black Dog Press.

"Calling Muzi (1971–1986) by Robert Peterson is reprinted from *Waiting for Garbo: 44 Ghazals*, copyright 1987 by the author, Black Dog Press.

"Grandmother's Onion Sandwiches" by Bernice Rendrick appeared in *Matrix*, 7/86.

"Blue Rock" by Adrienne Rich is reprinted from *Your Native Land, Your Life: Poems*, copyright 1986 by the author, W.W. Norton Company.

"Monterey Bay" by Gaël Rozière is reprinted from *Witness to a Landscape*, copyright 1986 by the author, PeerAmid Press.

"Snowfall" and "Tuis Ka" by Timothy Sheehan are reprinted from *Here*, copyright 1981 by the author, Brandenburg Press.

"Eve" by Marjorie Simon is reprinted from *Adam and Eve etc.* with George Fuller, copyright 1981 by the authors, Jazz Press.

"In Which I Get Very Little Help from My Friends" by Phillip Slater is reprinted from *How I Saved the World*, copyright 1985 by the author, Grove Press.

"Below Mount T'ui K'oy, Home of the Gods, Todos Santos Cuchumatán, Guatemalan Highlands" and "Signature (V)" by Joseph Stroud are reprinted from *Signatures*, copyright 1982 by the author, BOA Editions.

"The Heart's Education" by David Swanger appeared in *Poetry Northwest*, 1984.

"Taking a Photo" by Robert Sward is reprinted from *Movies: Left to Right*, copyright 1983 by the author, Southwestern Ontario Poetry.

"Eating Wild Mushrooms" by Gary Young is reprinted from *In the Durable World*, copyright 1985 by the author, Bieler Press. "At San Vicente Creek" by Gary Young appeared in *Cumberland Poetry Review*, 1983.

CONTENTS

INTRODUCTION

For an area with a population of 175,000, Santa Cruz possesses an extraordinary number of writers. The town started to attract literary people in the 1960's, and the mixture of progressive community, and lambent beauty of the setting continues to form a creative center of gravity.

With the number of writers now living here, putting together this book arose as a natural development. A local anthology has never been done. And the quality of work deserves attention.

The poets and authors in *Lighthouse Point* are the backbone of a vigorous literary scene. This year (1987–88) four reading series are offered in town, sponsored by Local 7 of the National Writers' Union, Louden Nelson Community Center, the University of California at Santa Cruz, and In Celebration of the Muse. The Muse readings have run for seven consecutive years, while Local 7's have run four years. On radio, Morton Marcus and Joe Stroud host a weekly poetry program which they inherited from Stephen Kessler and Gary Young. Young's press, Greenhouse Review, publishes out of the Santa Cruz mountains. More toward the center of town is Felicia Rice's Moving Parts Press. George Fuller's Jazz Press has been in operation twelve years, and in the south county Nick Zachreson runs Blackwells Press. A number of presses have recently set up shop here, including Robert McDowell's Story Line Press, Black Dog Press, New Society Publishers, HerBooks, Crossing Press, and M Press. Among the magazines winging out from the county are: George Fuller's *Poetry: Santa Cruz*, Nathaniel Mackey's *Hambone*, Stephen Kessler's *Alcatraz*, Joe Drucker's *Ally*, Robert McDowell's *Reaper*, and Candida Lawrence's *Coydog Review*. Recently defunct is George Hitchcock's *Kayak*. U.C.S.C. produces *Quarry West* and *Chinquapin*, while Cabrillo College distributes 12,000 free copies of the rousing *Porter Gulch Review*.

Three of the largest literary events ever held in the U.S. took place at the Santa Cruz Civic Auditorium. The Santa Cruz Poetry Festivals in 1974, 1976, and 1982 were masterminded by Jerry Kamstra, and writers like Kay Boyle, Amiri Baraka, Charles Bukowski, Floyd Salas, Allen Ginsberg, and Dianne di Prima drew audiences of 1,800.

In addition to its size and vitality, the literary scene here shows another unusual characteristic: it is hybrid. Every writer in the anthology moved here from somewhere else. Even for California these are exceptional demographics. While U.C.S.C. and Cabrillo first drew artists to the area, now the sense of a place apart, cupped between mountains and sea, creates its own gentle hold.

Also noteworthy about these writers is that a majority came of age during the tumultuous decade, the 1960's. It's an intriguing bit of irony that the subject which gains deepest attention from this group, whose generation was noted for rebellion and protests, is family.

The writers you read in these pages generally have earned local or national reputations. Lucille Clifton, William Everson, Tillie Olsen, and Adrienne Rich are eminent literary figures. We're honored to have them in the anthology and the community. Yet the lesser known and the unknown writers also present work capable of knocking off your knickers.

The one unfortunate aspect of editing this anthology was being unable to include all the serious writers in the area. We regret that people have been left out of the book.

Women writers form a major component of the literary community in Santa Cruz. Their contribution over the last decade is marked by the attendance and longevity of the Muse readings, the proliferation of writing workshops by and for women (first led by Ellen Bass, later Maude Meehan and others), and the camaraderie and support among women writers. These attitudes carry over to the community at large and provide welcome unity to a previously disparate literary scene. Women writers also foster the craft elements of passion, personalized voice, and political perspective.

Santa Cruz conspires to feed artists in a particular way. As Jim Houston explains, our unique southern facing coastline with wilderness to the north and open sea to the south stimulates and releases the creative imagination. For Santa Cruz's hybrid writers, the release of imagination means that their work takes off in dozens of directions. Indeed, when we were looking at the initial submissions, the lack of what could be called regional writing had us concerned. But in receiving William Everson's narrative poem, Gaël Rozière's lyric of Monterey Bay, and Maude Meehan's place poem, the power and innocence of redwoods, rising mountains, and Pacific Ocean took form.

Beyond Santa Cruz, the works range to Greece, Poland, Japan, Lebanon, Chiapas, West Point. This generation which cut its teeth on Vietnam has chosen the globe as its focus.

The writing in *Lighthouse Point* illuminates this time we inhabit, and the internal and cultural landscapes that determine our lives.

— *Steve Wiesinger*

FRANCISCO X. ALARCÓN

A Small but Fateful Victory

that summer night
my sister said
      no
she was not going
to do the dishes
anymore

my mother only
stared at her
maybe wishing
she had said
the same thing
to her own mother

she too had hated
her "woman" chores
of cooking cleaning
always looking after
her six brothers
& her father

a small thunder
shook the kitchen
while we quietly
looked at each other
around the table of
five other brothers

the sudden impasse
was broken when
my father put on
an apron & started
to run the hot
water in the sink

I could almost hear
the sweet music
of victory
        ringing
in my sister's ears
in my mother's smile

Carta a América

perdona
la tardanza
en escribirte

a nosotros
nos dejaron
pocas letras

en tu casa
nos tocó
ser tapetes

a veces
de pared
pero casi

siempre
estuvimos
en el piso

también
te servimos
de mesa

de lámpara
de espejo
de juguete

si algo
te causamos
fue risa

en tu cocina
nos hiciste
otro sartén

Letter to America

sorry
for the lag
in writing you

we were left
with few
letters

in your home
we were cast
as rugs

sometimes
on the walls
but almost

always
we were
on the floor

we served
you as
a table

a lamp
a mirror
a toy

if anything
we made
you laugh

in your kitchens
you turned us
into another pan

3

todavía	even now
como sombra	as a shadow
nos usas	you use us
nos temes	you fear us
nos gritas	you yell at us
nos odias	you hate us
nos tiras	you shoot us
nos lloras	you mourn us
nos niegas	you deny us
y a pesar	and despite
de todo	everything
nosotros	we
seguimos	continue
siendo	to be
nosotros	us
América	America
entiende	understand
de una vez:	once & for all:
somos	we are
las entrañas	the insides
de tu cuerpo	of your body
en la cara	on our faces
reflejamos	we reflect
tu futuro	your future

4

CHARLES ATKINSON

Plum

Try to recall what it's like
after a day's work in July
to bite into a ripe Mariposa,
dark clear through, almost
freestone and running with juice.

It's not the taste, at first,
but the surprise at finding
a sphere the color you'd have
chosen yourself—blood-rich.

Here it is, deepest summer
and this its marker come almost
without asking, and you laugh to be
here and not where you'd hoped.

And what if days are shrinking
and doubt's coming on and the regret
of not caring better for your life,
letting small pleasures die
before they're even born?

You had nothing to do with this one—
not friends, not even yourself
to thank for tending it—
but here it is, filled to the skin,
come into your palm without help.

It's not just sweet, not
just to quench a thirst.
It's a season. A short life.
A joy that needs nothing.

The rounded world is cradled
and felt for once,
and if a plum's like this,
then what can be wasted?

Take it now, and eat—
this smallest other you found
and taste, dripping down your cheek
and into your palm
all its runny happiness.

ELLEN BASS

Thanksgiving at Two and a Half

In the back pew
seated between her father and me
    as the organist accompanies the clarinet, precisely
    through Beethoven's sonata
she sings
softly—her grandparents do not hear—
Give my regards to Broadway
Remember me to Herald Square.

In the Photograph

for Janet and Sara

In the photograph
there is flour all over. White,
the unhealthy bleached kind. This is to be a birthday cake
and there has been enough of being sensible.

There is powdered sugar, bowls, measuring spoons, and melted
　　chocolate.
There is chocolate on the child's face and up her arms
and flour like a dusting of snow down the front of her red dress
　　　　which was her mother's red peasant blouse
　　　　　　and which she, the child, confiscated from the give-away pile.
　　　　It needs tucks which the mother will sew before the party.
It is the child's birthday — her sixth.

The woman in the photograph holds the strainer.
　　　　She was appalled when she found cake mix and canned
　　　　　　frosting
　　　　in the grocery bag. Her exact words to the mother were:
　　　　　　　　　　　　"You bought this crap?"
Now her hands are floured white and she has an intent expression
on her face. She resists smiling into the camera.
She is not opposed, though. Just the other day
　　　　she spoke of how important photographs were, how
　　　　as a child, she pored over those of her own mother.
　　　　"You should take pictures," she told the mother,
　　　　"to record these times, how you are now, for the child."
Wisps of hair curl against the angular planes of her face.
If anyone looks closely, it is clear she is handsome.

The child smiles into the camera.
It is one of those perfect smiles
not the school-picture grimace.
Her cheeks round as peaches, hair falling thickly to her waist.
Her eyes shine a little red from the flash and her hands are
    blurred.
She's clapping. At the moment recorded, they are open
fingers spread with glee.

The mother, of course, is taking the picture.
She slipped away for the camera when the red dress,
the white flour, the smell
of the chocolate, the squeals of the child, the calm
lake of the woman's face coalesced in her heart.

When the child searches the album for her mother's life
she will find many smiling poses,
but this one, perhaps, in which she does not even appear
is a truer self-portrait of her joy.

BARBARA BLOOM

The Honeymoon

In the morning, we saw
how the bear's muddy paws
had touched all the cars
right at the door handles
like the mark of a large hand
except for the pointing of the claws.
One car had been entered,
the back window broken
and food scattered all around.

All this, while we slept,
or tried to, in the narrow cot,
cold under the wool blankets,
trying to fit our bodies
not just against each other,
but into the idea
of always,
our breath marking the cold air white
for the briefest instant.

The bear must have loved
everything we eat!
Perhaps there were two of them,
opening oranges,
eating salty crackers,
and thick bars of chocolate,
while the sharp mountain air
wrapped around them,
and the swollen river roared so loud
even the noise of their feasting
became a silent blur.

Luther Burbank Gardens

Running my hands over the smooth
leaves of the cactus,
I remember my father told me
how Burbank talked to the cacti,
explained to them
that they no longer needed their thorns:
he would protect them now.
Scientists could not understand
how he developed this spineless variety,
and he did not tell them
about those walks at night
through the gardens
whispering to the plants,
how they listened to him,
knew the truth of it,
and willingly shed their spines.

CLAIRE BRAZ-VALENTINE

Cream of Wheat

Empty shelves,
father gone,
other woman.
Holes in shoes,
don't answer door,
bill collectors.
Go to church every Sunday.

Never mind.
Mama's here,
reading Uncle Wiggily,
make some Cream of Wheat.

Brush her hair
brown hair
brown like nuts
brown like tree bottoms
like good earth
with the scent of beauty.

Mama of the kitchen every day
and the ironing board
and the bills she cried over
and the woman
yes the woman
the other one
let's not speak of her.

Mother
and the laughter
with sister Sally
who brought the wreath cakes
and the stories that we loved.
And Anne the sister
with hair of silver.

Mama
with the babies at her breast
that I wanted,
Mama of the books and the baseball,
and a rampant fear of spiders,
Mama who listened
no matter for anything,
who heard.

Gate opener.
Light bearer.

WILFREDO Q. CASTAÑO

Full Electric Goddess

To Alma

I woke with the taste of Sunday
diesel engines coughed smoke and noise on the street
But—in me I had the taste of Sunday
Slow waking
My cock furrowing gently on the sheets
I wanted to lean my head in my hands and be photographed
I wanted to walk in the park with freedom and tigers
with Sunday in my soul tasting itself
Before the mirror I see my regeneration
I am a banana (I am a green chili pepper)
I am a quartz watch tacking electricity to the wall
I woke with the taste of Sunday fresh on my tongue
My vision fresh of you in the new white nightgown
your mother gave you—your thighs contasting the lacy cotton
with the lust of me and your smell and your brown skin
memorizing me until all my blood gathered
in my memories of our fucking
I wake with Sunday tasting me
I wake with children singing arm in arm
I wake with the camouflaged sun
The singing of the words that last night slept in the ink
This aromatic motorcycle called my heart heals, heals itself
beating-thumping-thumping-all night
Did the words think me—I say—did the words think of me?
It doesn't matter—it matters only when you dream (it always
    matters)
I must tell you—last night I spoke with the angels
and they were me
Last night I grew wheat and love and sent it to the starving
Last night I bathed in full electric goddess
The good good sleep—I died for seven hours and
woke with Sunday on my tongue.

LUCILLE CLIFTON

This Anger, This Grief

after the birth
of the second daughter
winnie mandela's womb
prepared itself for sons.

this grief
this anger
some of this
is the sons of winnie
mandela.

To My Last Period

i hated the mess
you made of things
woman. thirty-eight years
and you never arrived,
heavy in your red dress,
without trouble for me
some way, some where.

but now all that is over
and i feel like the grandmothers who
after the hussy has gone
sit holding her photograph
and smiling; "wasn't she
beautiful, wasn't she
beautiful?"

FLORINDA COLAVIN

Stripping the Limbs

<u>1</u>

Braced in the thick limbs of her trunk he stands
saw in hand
her old branches a tangle of neglect.
Today is the day my father has decided
we will prune her.
She stands in my yard.
He does not ask permission.

He cuts into her
swift with a vigor that belies his 73 years.
I swallow my protest at his blunt attack.
Hour after hour he works.
I haul away load after load of debris.

I do not apprentice myself to his skill
   do not wish to learn his brusque ways.
I watch from the ground as he carefully seals each wound
with black pitch.
She is naked.

<u>2</u>

Tiny red-green buds begin
I count each slender shoot as they reach sunward.
Day after day more appear
until too numerous to count.
By July she grows so rich with narrow green leaves
pepper-red flowers, sunlight no longer penetrates.

"The tree is so full of leaves I can't see through her."

"Nothing is going to stop that old tree," he says.
"Did you think she wasn't coming back?"

I do not admit my doubts.

3

Three months later, my father drops to the ground paralyzed.

4

Tears streaming down his face.
He concentrates on every move of my mouth
struggles to reproduce the word.
Time and time again it eludes.
A single sound so clearly formed in his mind
emerges as babble.
I am shaken to my roots.

5

A thousand single leaves
scattered in a fierce wind.

Clinging to her thick branches
I prune
with unskilled ignorant hands.
Gently I press pitch onto these cuts
but even its thick blackness
cannot completely seal her jagged wounds.
I pray my inept work
does not leave her
vulnerable,   unable to regenerate.

JOSEPH DRUCKER

The Painting of Blue Rivers

The long sleep's
hibernation of the non-thought,
   the sluggish mouth taste.
The rising of the sun like a blob
   of frowsy oil dripping
from a dirty sky.

On the mantelpiece,
my idle flute was woven beyond
   recognition into a silken
blanket by my hosts: the happy
   spiders.

I exhumed
the instrument, dusted it, then
   played sonatas and fugues
by Bach and Beethoven, hoping
   the music will scatter
the freeze into a seminal Spring.

But I felt
altogether ragged, depressed, as
   if I were keyed
surreally to a c minor symphony
   for immature, blubbered
   minds.

I vowed
to adjust my vision away from
   the crude, unimaginative;
vowed, also, not to degrade or
   stifle myself, nor remain
vulnerable to chance, but to make
   every effort

to neuter
my inner power structures, launch
        a serious campaign to
explore the greed, the cunning, of
        people around me, expose
them for what they were: dwarf
        spirits devoid of
        moral strength.

    When finally
my cat came to me yawning
        beautifully, I raised
my eyes to the night, astonished
        to behold how silence
was painting blue rivers across
        the starless void.

WILLIAM EVERSON

Renegade Christmas

Full moon at the solstice:
The head of the month and the heel of the year
Graze as they pass—incongruent syzygy.
The feminine principle prevails,
A reversal of roles. It behooves the wise
To walk warily.

                But the night glides without mishap.
Under the moon the sheer exaltation of loveliness
Suffuses the world.

                Then deep toward dawn
A gaggle of coyotes perched on the hill
Serenades moonset, a shivering ululation,
Suddenly to break and hang suspended,
The startled silence that swallows sound.

Out on the road our cross-breed elkhound
Roars in response, lawfully invoking the territorial imperative
Against the call of the wild.

                The coyotes sing back,
Arcane variations on the primal theme,
An evolving line of canine invention
Casting its spell on the listening night.

Once again the elkhound's challenge
Splits the silence, but this time uncertainly.
Something has touched him, some insidious affinity,
Aslink in his genes, betrays itself,
A quavering falsetto that gathers as it grows,
Subverting the measure of human fealty
To the wolf-pack in the blood.

For a time they contend,
The relentless torsion of opposed loyalties
Contorting his voice,
From whine to moan to incipient yelp.
Then all succumbs, domestic devotion
Capitulates to instinct,
Rustily joining the virtuoso performance
High on the hill.

I climb from bed
And look wonderingly out. He sits in the yard,
Muzzle pointed skyward as if baying the moon.
Never have I heard such unspeakable perturbation
Wrung from the throat, an atavistic intrusion
Gusting the heart.

Up on the hill
The listening coyotes laugh themselves silly,
Jubilant at the tell-tale ambivalence
Tormenting the dog. Then he is gone.

The movement of brush
Marks his passage up the canyon slope,
As a surface ripple charts the zigzag course
Of a foraging carp.

The rout is complete.
In his mad dash uphill he sloughs
Ten thousand years of domestication
In search of his soul.

* *

He is gone for two days.
I remark to my wife, "It looks like the gods
Claim another victim."

She considers this,
Pursing her lips, then decides against it,
"He'll come home."

And so he does.
This evening near dusk a scratch at the door.
I am all alone, and when I let him in
He goes straight to his corner,
Not greeting me, and curls up in a ball,
Nose tucked to tail.

But when my wife returns
He rises at once and goes to her, tongue lolling,
Half closing his eyes in a way they have
Seeking satisfaction.

She brings him his food,
And he wolfs it, ravenously, then flops in his corner,
Insensible with fatigue. Soon I hear him
Whine in his sleep, muscles twitching, every instinct alive
As he chases Coyote Woman through the moonlit glades,
Pursuing his dream.

I step out in the dark,
Look up at the stars in the crystalline night,
Brittle with frost. I think of Coyote Woman,
Snug in her den, the clot of the god
Alive in her vitals.

Tomorrow is Christmas Eve.
"Why, O God, do you do as you do?"
The question is moot: only the wonderment
Is real.

Back in the house
I poke at the fire. Beyond the bedroom door
My wife is asleep, no God-clot
Wakening her womb.

In the fire's last light
I say my prayers and tally my sins,
Such as they are, then make for bed.

Suddenly I hear Coyote Woman sing on the hill.

Curled in his corner
Elkhound raises his head,
Listening.

Coyote Woman
Cries again, the wild and careless
Inexhaustible joy
Of life resurgent.

Elkhound
Lowers his head between his paws
And takes up his dream.

GEORGE FULLER

Your Shirts

I see you as a boy in frozen Iowa
crossing an icy lake
with your two older brothers,
Lynn and D.D.
You, playful,
skate around their cautious steps.
I see you in Texas — seventeen —
lying by one year
to join the Air Force,
1915.
"Mad Canadians" you'd tell
"We'd lose one or two a week,
they'd try to fly under bridges."
I see you in Kansas City
in a blue double-breasted suit
at the Savoy Hotel
where years later I would go
remembering your stories.
I see you in Tulsa
shaking hands with loyal men,
later rubbing sleeves
with thin women in California.

Now I wear your shirts
monogrammed GEF,
carry around the lives you lived
in my pockets.
These shirts stand me up straight
while the frost of a Winter
70 years later
sets in, and the days get shorter.
I imagine you, in your father's shirts,
on that lake surrounded by cornfields
skating between
your slender brothers
in glassy days
I cross to with my eyes.

The Root Salesman

By comparison
I could be a root salesman.
What then?

My shoes muddy
by profession,
black mud
beneath my fingernails.

Fuchsia and hollyhock,
these are not my domain.
I would bring you beautiful
twisted carrots,
turnips, and mistress
of the underground,
the onion.
I would come to you full,
so very full
of good things to taste.
What then?

A salesman sells himself,
shoes just by standing,
happening to fit your feet,
just luck.
But only a root
can sell a root,
that's what I say.

About the tangle
along my neck and spine?
Skein of more than hair
that smells like salt
and must, matted
along my arms
which reach out to you.
What is it? you say.
Doll of dolls, I say,
come to me from the
furry rat cellar,
out of the iron-blue earth.
Doll of dolls, I say,
come and wrap me.
What then? you ask again.

Why only the prayer given to sailors,
I answer,
all things must have roots.

JAMES B. HALL

Old Man Finds What Was Lost

That time was in Ohio long ago when people lived on farms and did the work themselves but had electric lights inside the rooms and a radio to get the News and tractors and many well-known animals such as cows. Also many dogs in the farmyard all barking and running around in circles.

Farmer and Old Woman lived and worked on just such a farm; for many a year it was corn, hogs, wheat, and soybeans or maybe clover. Once they had children about the house, but not anymore as three daughters, each in turn, went off to live a better life in Cincinnati.

One August about midnight Farmer stood on his front porch and looked out across his ninety-two acres of corn and heard the corn growing, making springy little noises in the dark, clear back to his woods. Farmer looked once at the sky and then he locked all outside doors, but did not go very fast upstairs to where their bed was.

First, as was customary, Farmer turned off the electric light and then took off all his clothes and then laid hisself down beside Old Woman.

—Hotter, Farmer said, than a half-fixed fox in a forest fire.

Even when he didn't know it, Old Woman understood everything about Farmer; therefore, his remark told Old Woman what was on Farmer's mind—maybe.

As that thought was some real change in things, Old Woman decided to find out the lay of the land.

Old Woman half-rolled over to Farmer's side and she placed her leg almost on top of his leg. Old Woman felt she had the rights of it because Farmer hisself first mentioned fox.

Very softly Old Woman said into the pillow beside Farmer's ear, "Hooo?"

In times past when Farmer was young or had just returned from the stockyards with money or of an afternoon walked through his barns to view breeding stock or if the corn was well along, then he nearit always said,

—Hooo, yourself . . . ? and then in various ways the job got done, and that was that.

In the past there had been some real Hoooing around. But lately not much, which is what is being said.

As was natural, Old Woman understood Farmer was getting on in years. Moreover, the three girls were no longer about the house, taxes were up some, the neighbors talked drought, drought, and of recent date a blood virus taken down two shoats per week, all of which signified losses for everybody.

Well, this very day, Old Woman, herself, had done no work— except a little fancy tatting. She skipped the News and went direct upstairs full well knowing Farmer was soon to follow as he did not much like to be alone in the rooms of their house. Old Woman had something on *her* mind.

—I pass, Farmer said, and for the first time in his life felt bad to renege—the corn being so well along. To renege made him feel unnaturally old. Farmer had well-noted Old Woman tatting fast all afternoon, so knowed he was in for it.

Old Woman did not say anything at once for she understood his remark might be natural for a man of his years, though otherwise healthy and of good appetite.

Nevertheless, three months of I Pass was a considerable time. So Old Woman retch over and with her hand slid down the nice black hair of Farmer's belly. With her hand sometimes, as in play, she would find it and then take aholt of his business.

This time no business. Nothing—so to speak—for Old Woman to take aholt of.

—That's why I passed, Farmer said, and he was put out to let her know. Seems I lost it. Lost . . . my business.

Again Old Woman said nothing. But since she knew all of that territory very well, had looked it over many a time in broad daylight, she just very gentle, gentle searched around. Just looking for herself with her woman hand.

Old Woman was also some surprised. As Farmer claimed, there was not much; in fact, nothing in the whole territory.

Then Old Woman whispered very kindly in his ear, "Well, let's just see about this," and before Farmer could say I, Yes, No nor Flour, why out of their bed she sprang and turned on the electric light and—bang—she pulled back their coverlet.

And that was that.

For Old Woman to see him like that was always a sight: good legs and arms, and those shoulders, and his face maybe a little creased from the work and the sun as though afloat on the clean sheets, and ifn he opened those eyes, they was blue as an ocean.

Very closely, she inspected the whole territory, a thing which even under the circumstances gave some trifle of pleasure. Then she turned out the light, got back in bed, and caused herself to lie down next to Farmer. Hooo, she said, it's some little thing. Besides Hog Futures are steady, the girls are happy in Cincinnati, and your corn is well along. Tomorrow I'll kill us a chicken, largely for the dumplins.

In his mind, Farmer saw what she said in clear pictures. There was much to be thankful for, so after the chicken wouldn't they just rock on the porch and listen to the corn grow?

Old Woman went to sleep and then Farmer went to sleep— called it a day.

Well, no change in the Hooing, but Old Woman saw Farmer look everywhere: looked in the little tool box under the seat of the wheat binder; among sacks of clover seed because of the sweet, attracting smell; looked under the Leghorn hen because of her steady warmth, but nowhere around the place was his business to be found.

Not found, not mentioned, was Old Woman's thought and besides, twixt her and the gate post, she understood nothing was really lost; gradually it had become smaller and smaller, and now it was back where it came from. So at this moment it was at hand, in Farmer's belly. So to Old Woman it boilt down to this: salt the cow to get the calf, for she knew of old that it was never out never up.

In her ways, Old Woman was very smart, so the morning after Labor Day, as was her plan all along, she lay abed. No reason stated.

Come noon and Farmer went to the bedroom to see about it, there being no dinner cooked.

Still Old Woman faced the wall: taken her bed.

Four days passed and no meals forthcoming, so towards noon Farmer was back again to the bedroom and in effect said, We ought to Doctor. We ought to Doctor some.

"No Doctoring," Old Woman said very bravely. "It's too much money." Which was a point.

Four more days passed, and no change. Mostly to get things organized, and also because Old Woman could be stubborn as the off-mule in a sorghum mill, in effect Farmer said, You will have it, so I'll fetch the Bailey girl from town. She can look to your needs and cook some, and how much all-found a week oughten I offer her mother?

"Whatever is right," Old Woman said, and faced the wall.

So next day, from town, up pulls Farmer in his automobile and he parks it in the center of the barnyard.

Farmer gets out. He walks him around the radiator, and he open *her* door. Out steps this Bailey girl: all found, and wearing a starched, all-white uniform borrowed of her mother (also betimes a practical nurse).

Then all Billy-bedamned braked loose in that barnyard: dogs barking and running in circles; the yellow she-cat and half her litter a-streaked for the crib; Jim-the-Crow calling *Hey-Petey, Hey-Petey* from the grape arbor; the two mules poked their heads out the hogpen winders.

That Bailey girl were a lot better framed than most. Also a redhead. Also in the wind of the ruckus, holting down her dress hem with one hand, that Bailey girl's all-white uniform roilt up everything.

All of which signified not much in the bedroom, in private, when Old Woman laid out the work expected:

"Some light housekeeping," Old Woman said, and sat up real sprite on the edge of her bed. "But don't feed too heavy."

The Bailey girl took Old Woman's meaning: easy on the meat.

"And this next is betwixt just the two of us: though active, Farmer has got two failings. One, the left ear is not quite deef as a fence post. Second, his sight. Things close at hand he can not see too good—like handtools, or a knife and fork. Naturally, Farmer has his pride so he never lets on. Even to me."

"That's why," Old Woman continued, "Farmer is your real patient, but pretend it is me. Stay plenty outside with him, and from time-to-time I'll get my own tea water."

The Bailey girl took Old Woman's meaning: speak up to the left ear; help find little things at hand; keep a shut mouth, especially to Farmer.

"All correct," said Old Woman, and began to straighten up her bed.

Meanwhile Farmer was gone to the barn to see why two mules poked their heads out of two winders of a brood sow's pen.

Inside bright and early for two weeks it was a redhead and a white uniform in the kitchen. It was "Here's you aigs—no bacon, it's too dear"; it was "Here's your coffee and your knife," and she took Farmer's hand and gentle found him his fork.

"Also," says the Bailey girl, and because Farmer flinched some she knew his hearing was some better, so she whispered real close, "And here's your napkun."

—Yes sir, Farmer said, and he thought, Napkun for breakfast?

For two weeks outside it was the Bailey girl helping Farmer, her white uniform now normal, the stock not roilt up. Farmer was looking for something, like a blind dog in a meat house. Naturally, Farmer couldn't exactly describe it to a stranger, so the Bailey girl did her best, fetched him bolts, a lynch pin, a staple puller, a clevis, and held them close to Farmer's nose and said, "Is this it?"

Course it never was.

Gradual, however, Farmer gave it up, and only slicked down some harness, greased all wagon axles, and cleaned some clover seed. But the Bailey girl was there, *handing* him every little thing, close, and sometimes more so.

Then Old Woman heard Farmer sing "Tenting Tonight" in the

privy, and his laid-by corn never looked better. From her upstairs winder, Old Woman saw a white uniform always by Farmer's side. Well she noted Farmer was getting lively, and more so, which is what is being said.

So: the Bailey girl is in the corn crib. To get something dropped, she laid herself down and she rotched between some sacks of clover seed, stretch out cross-wise in her white uniform on the sacks.

Suddenly Farmer went outside to relieve hisself. And, well, there it was. Back in the same territory: he found his business.

Farmer came running back to the crib — to tell someone the news. He saw the Bailey girl laid out on the clover sacks and Farmer just couldn't help hisself. He pinched her. Right there. On the uniform.

The Bailey girl come up off the clover sacks like a she-cat at weaning. She cuffed Farmer. On his good ear.

"If I want my ass pinched," she yelled, "I'll get it done in town and I quit."

So the Bailey girl packed her jockey box and Old Woman paid her off and Farmer drove her back to town no words spoke.

Back home Old Woman was hard at it: smoke in the kitchen, and a nice fryer in the pan.

"Good riddance," Old Woman said without hard feelings; "Hired help is never the same and she wasn't feeding you anyways near enough meats. And I knew it."

Old Woman began to hum a song over the stove and everything was organized and back to normal.

That night in their bed, right away, Farmer said "Hooo . . . " and Old Woman said "Why Hooo, your self—."

And the job got done. And for some time there was plenty of Hoooing on the old home place in one way and another.

Though never so much as mentioning the Bailey girl again, the Old Woman thought this: it helped Farmer over a little drought and she, herself, got some much needed bedrest. So the expense was just about fifty-fifty, and it might be called Doctoring. Besides, they had never talked Florida vacation or anything like that.

What is general knowledge, howsomeever, is this: a few years later, whilst weeding an iris bed, Old Woman just died. Soon thereafter

Farmer died of a broken heart because he couldn't stand being alone in the rooms of their house.

Also general knowledge: the three daughters came home and naturally put the land, the stock, and all machinery to public auction. Jim-the-Crow went back to the woods; bids on all livestock was stronger than expected.

The daughters settled their three shares with no hard feelings and went their separate ways back to the City.

And that is how Farmer found what was temporary lost.

GEORGE HITCHCOCK

Antebellum

Inside the embassy the epaulettes meet
To edit each day the latest lying pact;
There buttons, gloves and shuffling feet
Gavottes of dust and Delftwork reenact.

This is the hour when crepitous in the breeze
All flags shall whip before red-ochre sleet;
The world's full up with stale geographies
And gazetteers addressed to trampling feet.

The metabolic scurvy spreads its dye
Throughout the tissue. The old disease
Unleashes shot-silk flowers in the sky.
Scrofulous rags inherit all our mysteries.

The siren telly lisps a song of death
Where all grenades implode back tenderly,
And drowned in blood the horse gives up its breath,
Its wayward bulging eyes fixed on eternity.

JAMES D. HOUSTON

The Dangerous Uncle

> If you would be unloved and forgotten,
> be reasonable.
> —from *God Bless You, Mr. Rosewater*
> by *Kurt Vonnegut, Jr.*

He was the renegade, the one who could not be tamed or domesticated, the wild card in the family. Was he my favorite uncle? No. But he was by far the most attractive, a man who could not hold his liquor or his money or any of the numerous women who passed through his life. Among my father's four brothers he was the closest in age, so they had grown up together in east Texas, Dudley and Anderson, companions and cohorts, two years apart. I have seen my father rigid with fury at something this brother had recently done to him. I have also watched him laugh as he recounted a boyhood stunt that foreshadowed the kind of life Anderson would lead. I mention this because my father was not what I would call an outgoing or expansive man. He was not given to shows of pleasure, yet Anderson could make him laugh aloud.

"I remember a day we were down along the creek," he told me once, "and back in that part of Texas the creek was the only place where you could cool off in the summer. I guess I was around twelve and Andy was around fourteen. He had this trick he liked to do, just to show off. He used to do it at school until the teachers made him quit. He was always real limber, you see. He had a way of putting one foot up behind his head, like a Hindu, and he was mighty proud of himself whenever he got his foot up there, since he was the only one in our family who could do that.

"Well sir, on this particular day, just about the time we had our shirts pulled off, but still had our trousers on, a couple of girls came walking along the creek trail. Anderson decided he would show them something they would never forget, and he commenced to shove his whole foot and ankle up behind his head. The girls saw that and they got to giggling and ran on down the creek. Anderson got to laughing so hard he fell over. He'd been standing on one leg, ya see, like a stork. For a while he was laying there in the dirt by the creek laughing till the tears ran down his face. Then he quit laughing and looked up at me with this funny look, and he said, Hey Dudley, come over here and give me a hand, will ya, while I get my foot down.

"I went over there and pushed and pulled a while, with him telling me what to do and where to grab hold. But it turned out there wasn't much either one of us could do because his foot was just plain stuck. He had shoved it over too far and got his neck turned some kind of way, and I had to leave him there and run back home to get my dad and our oldest brother, who was already grown, and stronger than anybody else too, because he did pushups and lifted weights, and bring them down there. It was a mile to the house and a mile back. Before we got near where he was we could hear Anderson yelling. His leg had cramped up. He thought he was going to die along by the creek bank with one foot locked behind his head."

The way dad told it, that was the prelude to Anderson's entire career — the family clown and a born nuisance, always leaving a mess behind that someone else had to come along and clean up. It was also the longest story I can remember hearing him tell. He was not a talkative man, yet he would talk about Anderson. I think he had to, there was so much to get off his chest. Anderson called things out of him no one else could call out. My dad was not given to shows of anger. Yet this brother could make him curse and slam a fist into the side of the house. He was not a violent man, but one day Anderson made him angry enough to kill.

This happened after we moved south into Santa Clara Valley, where dad had picked up a few acres with a house and outbuildings. During our years in San Francisco, before and after World War Two, one of his dreams had been to get out of the city and back to the land. In the late 1940s, the valley had not yet begun to expand and explode and become the high-tech headquarters it is today. It was still one huge orchard. Out near the western foothills we had a small piece of it, with some fruit trees, a barn, a greenhouse.

Not long after we made this move, Anderson started showing

up three or four times a year. He liked it there, since he shared dad's taste for the rural life. They shared a few other things too, but in certain crucial ways these two brothers were like day and night. Dad was a quiet and inward man. Anderson was a compulsive talker. Dad was anchored. Anderson was not. He had gone through five wives and countless jobs, and now he was drifting back and forth between Texas and California. Dad would allow him to stay, sometimes for months, because they had grown up together, and because he was the brother with nowhere else to go, and because Anderson would talk him into it, and because Anderson, when sober, was a man of many talents. Perhaps too many.

He was a carpenter. He was a gardener. He was a mechanic. He could sink postholes and erect a fence that ran straight and true. One summer I watched him take over a picking crew, become foreman for a rancher we knew, and get twenty acres of apricots gathered in record time. For a number of years before the war, Anderson made a good living as a hairdresser in Los Angeles. He changed his name to *Andre*, and he took advantage of the fact that in their boyhood section of Texas the nearest town of any size had been Paris. He became "An-dray from Par-ee." With his wavy hair and his rascal's grin and his gift of gab, it worked. He made and spent a lot of money.

When World War Two came along he joined the army and travelled the Pacific with a construction battalion, Hawaii, New Guinea, the Aleutians. The heavy drinking started then and led to a stomach ulcer that finally put him in an army hospital. No one could say it was the army or the war that disabled him, but he left the service with a disability pension and a chronic condition that had him moving in and out of V.A. hospitals for years. Mostly out. He wouldn't sit still for treatment. He would check himself in on a Monday. By Tuesday night he would be sneaking out the side door, carrying his shoes.

If medicine was prescribed, he wouldn't take it. If advice was given—such as Stop drinking—he would listen a while, then forget. Twice he joined A.A., and twice he backslid. By the time we were installed in Santa Clara Valley he was living on his pension checks, which he tended to blow as soon as one arrived in the mail. His monthly binge could end with a phone call from a bar in Salinas. Or it could be a call from an all-night service station in Reno, someone saying, "Mr. Houston? We got a fella here out of gas and out of money sitting in a vegetable truck that isn't his and he can't remember where he got it, who says you're his brother and not to call the police till we call you first . . ."

Dad would slam the phone down and say that as of today Andy would have to take care of himself because this was absolutely the last time he was going to bail him out of anything!

The next day they would both appear in the driveway side by side in our pickup, my dad stoic, the survivor who had come west during the 1930s with seven dollars in his pocket and now had seven acres with a house in the country, and Anderson, disheveled, hangdog, the prodigal brother with nowhere to lay his head.

We would soon learn he had promised dad something. We would usually learn it from Anderson himself, as we sat around the supper table. And I should point out that in those days I did not yet know the broken pattern of his life. I only heard his Southern Comfort voice, saw the crafty eyes of the garrulous uncle, the colorful uncle, the uncle you hoped would stay for a while.

"Some people are slow learners," he would say, as he dove into his first solid meal in a week, talking between mouthfuls of biscuits and gravy, pork chops, blackeyed peas. "And you people are looking at the slowest learner of all time. But I'll tell you right now, ol Andy has learned his lesson at last. I have taken my final drink. I swear it. Dudley here is my witness. You are all my witnesses. If it wasn't for Dudley, I would be a goner. I would be breathing my final breath in the darkest gutter of the skid rows of Los Angeles, and nobody knows that better than I do. I tell ya . . ."

Now tears would be glinting in his red-rimmed eyes, as he paid tribute to all the many ways my father had saved him from himself. "I tell ya, I am going to make it up to you, Dudley. I am going to make it up starting tomorrow. Starting tonight! We've got a couple of hours of daylight left. Soon as we finish supper I am going to go out there and get started on that chicken house roof. Yes sir.

I am gonna get a new roof on your chicken house, so them white leghorns will sleep cozy. Then I'm gonna run that fence down along to the end of the property line like I started to do last spring. And listen. Let me tell all of you right now, help me stay away from the mailbox. I mean it! I don't want to *see* that pension check. I don't even want to see a calendar. That way I'll lose track of time and won't know which day of the month it is and won't even know when to look for that check, because that check belongs to *Dudley!* You all hear me now? You are talking to a man who is making a fresh start!"

I should also point out that dad's vision of how things could look around the place ran far ahead of his available time. There was always brush to be cleared or the barn to be patched, a chimney to rebuild, a bedroom to add on, an acre of trees to prune. He was working fulltime as a painting contractor, and the weekends were never long enough. My mother meanwhile had her hands full managing the house, tending her flowers outside the house, keeping me and my sister in school clothes, and giving any spare hours to the vegetables. In this little world Anderson's skills were much appreciated, particularly when it came to the chickens, which played a key role in my father's dream. A well managed chicken pen would provide the eggs and the meat to complement the tomatoes and the corn and the greens that would emerge from the year-round garden. Building up his flock little by little, he had accumulated thirty white leghorns and a few Rhode Island Reds. He had recently widened the pen with new fencing. Anderson must have known, consciously or unconsciously, that the henhouse roof was right at the top of dad's long list of chores, and the very offer that would soften his heart.

So once again he stayed, and two months went by without incident. Fresh loam soon darkened all the flower beds. New gravel appeared in the driveway. Borders of brick and river-stones had encircled the fruit trees nearest the house. At night, around the table we would listen to him talk, and this in itself was worth a lot. Dad never talked much at the table. He ate in silence, thinking about what had to be done tomorrow.

Two months like this, then one night the supper table was quiet again. My father, home late and coming in from the garage just as the food was set out, looked around the kitchen and said, "Andy lost his appetite?"

My mother said, "I thought maybe he was with you today."

"Why would he be with me?"

"I sure haven't seen him around here."

He thought about this and started to eat. After a while he said, "What day is it?"

"Thursday."

"What day of the month?"

"The second."

He thought again and ate some more. "I suppose if you brought in the mail yesterday there is no way he could have got his hands on that pension check."

"I thought you brought the mail in yesterday," my mother said.

"How could I bring in the mail when I wasn't here."

"I told you I had to go shopping."

"You don't have to go shopping right when the mailman is coming up the road."

"I can't spend my whole life walking back and forth to the mailbox, Dudley."

This came out sharp. When he didn't respond, she softened. "One time that check didn't get here until the third or the fourth. The way he keeps changing addresses, it's a wonder it ever gets here at all."

"He wouldn't take off by himself if he didn't have any money."

"Did you look in your clothes closet?"

"I'd better do that," he said, pushing his chair back.

If anything was missing, a jacket, or one of dad's favorite shirts, it meant Anderson was gone and did not plan to return for quite some time. But nothing was missing, which meant the phone could ring at any moment. Dad sat down at the table again and pursed his lips and narrowed his eyes and looked out into the dusk, waiting for that call, already bracing for it.

For three days he waited, then he began to worry that something might have happened, something worse than drunkenness. On the night of the third day he drove around to the nearest saloons. No one had seen Andy.

The next afternoon I was out in front of the house trying to straighten the handlebars on my one-speed when he re-appeared, carrying what looked like a square cage. He wasn't staggering. He was very erect, walking with his shoulders back, planting his feet like a mountaineer starting a long climb, though there was no mountain. The road was flat.

He called out, "Jimmy! How you doin, son?"

"I'm doin fine, uncle Anderson. How you doin?"

"I got somethin for ya," he said.

As he approached, I looked again at the cage, trying to see through its close wire mesh. There was something alive inside, eager to get out. But that was not what he meant. From his scuffed-up leather jacket he withdrew a photograph and handed it to me with a wink. It was a folded and rumpled but still glossy eight-by-ten of a young woman in a skimpy white swimsuit, early Jayne Mansfield perhaps, or someone of her proportions. I don't have a clear memory of the face. I was fourteen, and I was transfixed by the cleavage. I glanced at Anderson and saw him watching my hunger, the depraved uncle, the outlaw uncle, the uncle you wished would take you somewhere.

He winked again. "I got somethin for your daddy too," he said, lifting the lid of the cage an inch to reveal a beak, a glittering eye. Half a head forced its way out, black and fierce. Anderson pushed the lid shut.

"Your daddy is big on hens, but he is short on roosters. This is a little rooster I picked up over in San Jose. Fella I ran into raises em to fight. So they got plenty of spunk. This little black one here is the spunkiest chicken I have ever seen. It is just what your daddy needs to pep up his flock. You know what I mean? Cross breeding is what I'm talking about. Hybrid vigor."

Though I knew next to nothing about raising chickens, even less about fighting cocks, I knew this sounded like a dangerous idea. I also knew better than to stand in his way. There was whiskey on his breath, and smoke in his clothes, and in his eyes a glint just like that rooster's, somewhere between mischief and madness. Once before, when he was this far along, he had challenged me to a fight. With clenched fists swirling he had demanded that I punch him as hard as I could, to try for the face. If I was afraid to punch my own uncle in the face, he had cried, I was a yellow-bellied coward and no nephew of his. Today he was on a kind of automatic pilot, he was walking and he was talking, but he was hearing no one, seeing nothing but some crazed vision of how this bird was going to transform his brother's flock — which of course it did.

Holding to his own straight and narrow course he moved past the house, past the barn, around a corner of the pen. Once inside the gate, he set the cage down on its side and unlatched the lid.

The cock rushed out, with an impatient lift of sleek black wings, so black, in late sun, the close-trimmed feathers had a purple tinge. As if surprised to find no adversary there, it stopped in the middle of the yard, muscular and nervous, its head twitching, its tense legs ready to spring.

Anderson had probably picked up that bird right after a fight. Spurs were still tied to its heels, little knives that looked dark with what might have been blood, though I wasn't sure. He only stood still a few seconds. These cocks that have been trained to kill, they must feed on fear. It must bring out the worst in them. The leghorns had scurried for the fence, clucking and bunching. This black rooster went for the other males first, then started after the hens, ripping and slashing, jabbing at eyes, sometimes lifting off the ground to drive spurs into a defenseless breast or wing or rump.

I remember Anderson poised in the half-open gateway, for a long moment of stupefied horror, while a few birds made their escape between his legs. He began to kick at them, warning, "Look out now! Look out!" Then he was a barnyard dancer, waving his arms at the flurry, shouting, "Hyeah! Hyeah!" Wary of the rapier beak, he made some half-hearted lunges. Finally he yelled at me to go inside and get my .22.

Loading it took a while. The rifle stood behind my desk. The shells were in another room, one dad kept locked. By the time

I came bounding through the back door, his pickup had pulled into the driveway. I watched him climb out and walk to the fence and gaze at what he knew was his brother's handiwork. Some birds had fluttered out the gate or into the safety of the henhouse. At least half were dead or badly wounded, flopping around with broken wings, broken backs, fluid running from a torn eye. It was a battlefield of feathers and carcasses, with one bird still on two feet, the spent but victorious killer cock, his black coat gleaming with blood.

For a silent minute dad surveyed this carnage. His teeth pressed together until the jaw muscles stood out like flat rocks inside his cheeks. Then he turned toward Anderson, sitting on the woodpile about twenty feet away with his face in his hands. Dad walked over to the chopping block, freed the hand axe and stood there until Anderson raised his head. Seeing the axe, he swallowed what he probably figured was going to be his final swallow.

Dad turned away and walked to the chicken pen and kicked open the gate and kicked leghorn carcasses out of the way. When he had the battle-weary rooster cornered, he grabbed it behind the neck in a grip so sudden and tight, the bird looked paralyzed. Squeezing it at arm's length, he brought it back to the block. This seemed to revive the bird, whose squirming life-fear, in turn, revived Anderson. Cold sober now, his face filled with pleading, he looked up and said, "Don't do it, Dudley."

The hand axe rose, and Anderson said it again. "Please don't do it. That rooster cost me fifty dollars."

"FIFTY DOLLARS!" my father shouted. "That's damn near half your pension check!"

"That's what I'm trying to tell you."

The axe fell with such force, the blade sank two inches into the wood, while the black head went one way, and the rest of the bird went the other. They watched it run in circles, with blood spurting from the open neck, until the life was spent and it fell over into the dirt.

Quietly my father said, "I want you to go get that bird and pluck it."

Tears were streaming down Anderson's face, tears of relief that he himself was still alive. He said, "Pluck it?"

"I want you to pull out every last feather, and that includes the real small ones underneath the wings and inside the legs."

"What for?"

"We're gonna eat that bird for dinner tonight. If it cost fifty dollars, we might as well get some use out of it."

"I tried to bargain that fella down, Dudley. I swear I did. But he just wouldn't listen. Fifty was his bottom offer."

Disgusted, my father stepped back into the pen, where he began to clean up the mess, salvage what he could. He sent me out to round up the strays. Anderson went to work on the rooster. About an hour later he presented it to my mother, who had come home from an afternoon's shopping to find her dinner menu slightly revised. She had cooked a lot of chickens, but never a fighting cock. She decided to boil it, and she let it boil for a long time, hoping for some kind of stew.

Late that night, when we sat down to supper, we discovered that boiling only made it tougher. In death as in life that bird was solid muscle. Though narrow strips of flesh could eventually be torn from the bone, they were unchewable. Several minutes of silent struggle passed before anyone dared to mention this.

With a hopeful grin Anderson said, "It's not that bad."

"I suppose I could have tried roasting it," my mother said.

"It's not that bad at all," Anderson went on, "considering the life this bird has led."

He winked at me and then at my sister, and we would have laughed, were it not for the cloud hanging over the table, which was the great cloud of my father's disappointment in the brother who had gone too far. Anderson knew this, even as he tried one more time to get a rise out of him.

"Fact a the matter is, what we're lookin at here is a fifty dollar dinner. Now I know you aint never had a dinner that was that expensive, Dudley. I'd say we're eatin mighty high on the hog tonight!"

Dad nodded. "I guess you're right, Andy. We'd have to drive clear to San Francisco to get a dinner that cost this much."

Anderson's laugh burst out, raucous and full of phlegm. He pounded on the table. "You kids hear what your daddy just said? We'd have to drive clear to San Francisco!"

His laugh filled the kitchen and went on for a long time, but all it drew from dad was a thin smile, a painfully courteous smile for the brother who had finally pushed him past his limit.

Years later we would all be able to laugh about that day, dad too, the way he laughed about the time Andy's foot got stuck behind his neck. I see now that Anderson had always been the one to do this for him, in a way no one else could—rile him, stir him, tickle his funnybone. But this time forgiveness was still a long way off. And it turned out to be the last night Anderson sat at our table.

As time went by, news would trickle our way, from other relatives who had taken him in, or invented reasons not to. For a while, as I heard the stories other had to tell, I thought dad had been too gullible, the way he had let Andy talk him into things year after year, then steal his clothes and his time and his trust. It's clear to me now that dad loved him more and had put up with his antics longer than anyone else had been able to.

I don't know what passed between them, in private, before he left, but he was gone the next morning, heading back to Texas, the dark uncle, the dangerous uncle, the uncle you never forget.

JEANNE WAKATSUKI HOUSTON

Fire-Horse Woman

a scene from a novel-in-progress
Kagoshima, Japan, 1905

Kajima Tadao sat in the small hut of the seamstress Sachiko, sipping tea, pleased to have been asked by the prominent Matsubara to act as go-between. Besides being flattered by the request from his childhood friend, he was curious to see the beautiful Kimiko. Her beauty was well-known throughout the countryside. And because her background was mysterious, rumors abounded. The logic of the peasants was that because she was unmarried, she must be unmarriageable, and although no one remembered any attempts or failures in setting up a match with her, stories flew that secret investigations had uncovered serious flaws: insanity tainted her family line; she was the mistress of a high-placed government official; she suffered from the dreaded and inheritable disease tuberculosis.

Sachiko poured another cup of tea for him and for herself. She had purposefully sat herself across from him so she could face the shrine on her *tokonoma*. She needed the support from her dead brother's spirit to help carry through her plan.

"As you know, Matsubara Seizo is looking for a wife for his son Hiroshi in America. He is the second son. But, Matsubara is treating him like an oldest son, because he feels he is starting a new family in America." He wanted the old seamstress to know that Matsubara was not following the tradition of primogeniture where the oldest son inherited everything. The second son would be a good catch, too.

He studied her face, politely avoiding direct contact with her eyes.

"Hai. I know about Matsubara's quest. Everyone in this village and miles around knows."

"Then you must be aware why I am here to see you." Kajima was anxious to get to the point.

"Hai. In fact, I am quite pleased for my niece Kimiko." She opened the way for discussion.

After reporting the basic background of the Matsubara family,

Kajima began talking about Hiroshi. "Hiroshi is doing quite well in America now as a farmer. The family hopes to start a *shoyu* manufacturing business there someday."

He then produced a picture of a serious-faced young man. He was clean shaven, and thick black hair lay slicked down on a narrow head. Sachiko liked the sensitive mouth and sad-looking eyes that looked out at her from the new photograph.

"He is thirty years old, born in the eleventh year of the Meiji."

Sachiko glanced over to the shrine. Did she catch a glint of light flickering off the gold painted filigree? Drawing in a deep breath, and cautiously veiling her eyes with inscrutable politeness, she proceeded to tell Kajima the carefully made-up background for her niece.

"Aha!" she started out. "What good coincidence! He was born in the year of the rabbit, no? Kimiko is twenty and born in the twenty-first year of the Meiji, which makes her ten years younger than Hiroshi. That is a good age span, don't you think?"

Kajima was pleased and somewhat surprised at Kimiko's age. The rumors were that she was older. He had heard twenty-four and even twenty-six. Obviously, it was her mature manner that conveyed this false deduction, he mused.

Sachiko continued, her courage bolstered by his pleased response to her first lie. "As you know, my niece is an orphan, the only daughter of my older brother. He was a fisherman and was lost at sea. His wife died soon after, from grief, I am sure." She let a tear slide down her cheek before she wiped it away with her kimono sleeve. This second lie came easier. An accidental death while working seemed more honorable than having been victims of a catastrophe caused by carelessness. Rather the sea gods had claimed her brother . . . not the raging inferno, sparked by a glowing cinder left irresponsibly undampered in a kitchen fire and fanned by the wind sweeping down the mountain into the snow covered valley. A smoking heap of ashes was all that had remained of Kodama Tsutomu, his wife and son, and their small house. The only surviving family member was Kimiko, who had been visiting relatives when the tragedy struck.

Kajima need not know about the fire. People would wonder why the family deserved such an ill fate. She didn't want Kimiko's past tainted with bad karma.

"Kimiko is very adept at sewing. As you know, I am a seamstress. She has been with me since she was a child, and I have tried to raise her as my own daughter. She is quiet, but not timid. Does Hiroshi-san have a forceful nature?"

Kajima blinked his eyes and hesitated for one telling moment, but recovered quickly to smile and slowly sip his tea. He realized he hadn't asked Matsubara about his second son's personality traits. This was turning out to be a most unusual go-between negotiation. But then, this *sashin kekon* thing was new, too. He ad-libbed.

"Yes, Hiroshi is quite strong-willed. Unlike most second sons he has a mind of his own and is quite independent." He guessed Sachiko wanted to hear that. Who cared if it was not true? They would be far away in America with no recourse, no one to blame. The thought encouraged him, and he began to elaborate upon Hiroshi's heretofore unknown character.

"He is also poetic and quite scholarly. He writes *tanka*. I understand he is learning the language of the *gaijin* and even knows how to drive those automobiles."

Sachiko nodded her head and allowed her eyes to widen with impressed amazement. "Ah, so . . . well, they will get along. Kimiko writes poetry, also. She has always been interested in books, and knows how to read. In fact, if she were a man, I am sure she would have made a way to go to school." She didn't have to make this up about her niece. Even as a small child, Kimiko had shown a literary bent, curious about *kabuki*, begging to learn how to read. It was fortunate her friend Hanako, the old retired geisha from Kyoto, had taken an interest in her and had taught her stories, how to sing, and even some elegant manners.

"And, as for her health, Kimiko is number one—no t.b. or insanity in the family, and no history of barrenness."

Relieved by the agreeable way in which the discussion was progressing, both Kajima and Sachiko relaxed and let their imaginations and tongues run wild with fabricated backgrounds for the young couple. They indulged themselves with fanciful talk, since both realized there would be no checking up or further investigation. They were free to create the perfect match, projecting upon the principals all those attributes and talents they wished had been their own.

When Kajima stood up to leave, the atmosphere was jovial and light. The emptied teapot might just as well have been a spent cask of sake.

"Now, what did you say Kimi-chan's sign is?" He was already referring to Kimiko in a familiar way.

"I believe she is an ox. The ox and rabbit are a very good match, so the gods are with us, it seems." Sachiko was beginning to believe herself the new background she had created for Kimiko. "Please convey to Matsubara-san my delight in uniting our families with this marriage. I know my brother and his wife, bless their souls, are pleased."

"Good." Kajima stepped outside the door. He wished Kimiko would arrive so he could see her at close range. But his wish was not to be granted that day, and he took leave of Sachiko, promising to be in touch soon again.

BARBARA HULL

The Children of Salvador

> The sorrow of the world
> is an image we fall into.
> — *Krishnamurti*

i. War

Children are abandoned in the hills.
It is against the law to look for them.

ii. Earthquake

He sells babies,
pulls them from under
their dead mothers.
He holds a crying child.
He says, this baby is yours.

He comes to me with another.
It is sick, covered with blood.
The mother lives with seven
children in the streets. No,
he says, this baby is yours.

He takes me to a hotel room.
He says, your baby is inside.
The mother is dead.

In the countryside,
he takes me to a marketplace.
A woman in a black shawl
is holding my baby.
The baby is dead.

iii. Orphanage

The children stay in tents in a field.
A priest says daily mass. The older children sing.
Nuns in white appear on TV holding babies.

A twelve-year-old girl fills plates with beans.
She thanks us for helping them.
They are afraid they will be forgotten.

iv. Home

The trees are filled with wild birds.
They cleave to the branches,
hold their wings to themselves.

Anniversary Poem: A Second Grieving

for my father, James Hull
died February 13, 1984

This time she will do it right.
There will be no drowning.
There will be a trip to the river.
She will see the fish under the surface.

She will be lifted in his arms,
and she will be dipped like a leaf in the water,
like a wave,
she will become translucent,
and she will feel her face in the warmth of his chest,
she will feel the hair on his chest
like warm moss,
and she will feel his hands and his fingers
along the back of her neck,
and she will weep,
and he will smooth her forehead.

She will see the red birds fly overhead
and dive into the water behind her
like a shaft of blood,
and it will wash over her,
and he will wash her in the wave of the river,
and it will be like a cloud turning blue.

She will see the mist inside her.
It will separate into parts,
and she will feel them lift away from her.
She will feel herself empty.
She will be nothing but light.

Like silk her skin is damp,
very white.
At the edge of the river
she waits.

PAULA JONES

The Touch Tank
Monterey Bay Aquarium

for Balin

I need love but do I have to
follow you around
my flat cheek in a crowd
turned to encounters?
I have reached into the tank
and touched the chiton   pried it
if it wouldn't have me
stroked its sucking leg   why not?
poked at the lugubrious sea cucumber
but I couldn't wait any longer
for you to find me.
Where were you
when I bent to pet the bat ray
who sidled up the wall?
Do you think it will be tamed
(wet velvet and not cold)
the way the sign said?
You were probably outside
watching the waves pile up
in the cavernous bay
not thinking about what
lies under.

STEPHEN KESSLER

Heart on the Chopping Block

The masseuse loosened my afternoon,
legs relaxed by the hands of a long woman
whose soup was brewing as I left her studio.
Gulls cruised, schools of fish
were swimming outside.

A seine of faces in the saloon —
one week done, and the man who yesterday fixed my car
beers up down the bar, many old friends
and enemies gossiping in the golden light.

In the world at last after long retreat —
how do you live?

Across the vaguely Arabian landscape
move acres of my tribes, my lost
kids from 6th grade waiting out the air raid
drill, and among these your face an oasis
come great distances to meet mine, sheltered,
and dine, forgetting our former diseases, your lover
left in a far land, the sad disappearances of our peers.

We talk, telling fortunes
in firewood, caution, almond
oil and the other anointments,
skin. So serious. How can I speak
of kissing you goodnight next to an old car.

Listening to George Coleman at Kuumbwa

Live this long in a town
and you see faces on the street you know
all the time,
catch glimpses of profiles you glanced from the side
long ago in a store
or danced with in a bar to a local band.
Tonight it's another club,
the sole chance you have to solo along with a master sax player,
listening and recollecting all at once
everything you lost in time.
Each day now feels more crowded with deadly duties,
every task too urgent to postpone on account of poetry—
life & death decisions you can't delay for art's sake
but must face: debts you never dreamed about
back in the soft suburbs,
payments you have now
to acknowledge and set down as a love letter
to the one at home.
This is how the afternoon's anguish
is eased, thru a reed
like the New Yorker's breathing,
urbanely building invisibly a disappearing portrait
of history played for ages in hot ensembles
and now leading his own
under a climbing moon.
It's a cool night,
two pairs of socks, black cap covering the spot
God wants to watch,
and the rhythm section doesn't even know the time,
they're slamming thru clocks & calendars
a fierce percussive fire,
swearing on a big city
how *bad* it is to be blowing away the chains
and getting back to some other land

where the song began.
I feel at home here
and far away, sending a wireless line
across all these houses and hills between us
hoping you hear something of my love.

EDWARD KING-SMYTH

The Chinese Doctor Learns to Drive

For him it was the first time
(after months of driving the coast road):
a sudden luminescence of eyes
trained to moon and stars, blinded
in the headlights, a *whunk* beneath the wheels,
and the brakes hit too late.

Between patients he replays it for us:
the U-turn; then hefting its dead weight
still warm, fingering the puffs of fur
behind each ear, the one leg snapped . . .
bobcat? or possum? he doesn't know.

He could not know how the buffalo
shied from crossing the trans-
continental railroad, their great
circular migration of the plains
broken, and how they died:
on the Kansas-Pacific line,
passengers emptied pistols into herds
that rubbed against the cars, then let
them lie. Their teeth were calcium
the roots of tall-grass prairie
had drawn through centuries-deep soil.
The Cheyenne, the Arapaho
danced to angry spirits
that had trapped the shaggy nomads
underground. Along the right-of-way,
bone gleamed through the carcasses.

But he'd gone back,
dug a rough grave with a stick
and made a cross.
Now he bandages the blisters on his fingers,
asks about the inland route home.

ROSIE KING-SMYTH

Summer Nights on the River Island

At bedtime I asked them,
the cousins younger than I.
We were up in the cubbyholes
under the eaves, with the old bear-rug smell
and the sound of pigeons cooing.
I carried them,
their smooth young bodies hugging mine,
fresh after baths, or warm from hide-and-seek,
tucked them in still nuzzling,
and as they fell asleep
urged them —
Can you remember
what it was like
before you were born? —
as if their newer flesh must hold the secret
mine somehow had lost,
and though their bodies pulsed with it,
I needed them to speak.
For I was listening from a far edge of childhood
where the moon-shadows lengthened,
and the night grew huge
with every rustle
of leaf,
and even the island was held
deep in the river-bed.

ROBERT LUNDQUIST

The Blood Myth

The blood of a woman and the blood of a horse
Are running through the field.

There is the odor of birth
There are the arrows of gull's feet to direct them

The blood of the woman teaches the blood of the horse her name

The woman reaches inside the horse to find
The body of a bird without shadow

The horse who is black finds fresh mint breathing beneath stone

The woman kneeling
Steals the eggs of a pheasant whose flight is trapped inside her

The gull's wing broken flies without sound.

Sometimes

Sometimes it is like a dream in which you drive through the night to visit your parent's home. When you arrive, there are cars in the driveway that should have left a year ago: your brother's, both your sisters'—they are young, stepping through shadow, frightened of moonlight.

Upstairs, only one of your parents is sleeping. The light above your mother's bed off white before dawn.

Turning to park in the street, forgetting the cello still tuned to Rastokovich lying in its case behind you, you stop; you hear people crying in their sleep, each disturbed by the sadness in their life.

Halfway home the branches cross in front of you. Bare limbs cover the street you are driving. Again you stop. On a porch a young boy speaks to his mother in the dark. You listen, remembering this time what it is behind you.

LYNN LURIA-SUKENICK

How to Sing at the Shore

There are two oceans: a front view of someone breathing evenly, and a side view of someone's enormous crying. And both are a woman. Her vowels are drowned angels, her consonants are wood gathered into bundles. Swim in her upper register, where you make your way with your hands, a stroking that never stops. This is singing; what did you think singing *was*? She'll change your blue suit to emeralds, she'll open your pursed lips. And if the emperor forbids all singing for a hundred years, her sweet waters and her bitter will raise you up and whisper, *Do what you want, do what you want, do what you want.*

How to Play the Harmonica at the Shore

First, you blow. You give your breath to the honeycomb, and all the notes you don't need you mask with your tongue. Play it like an ocean, a low-down horizon in your mouth, a surfy hymn. Take it from the top, from Atlantic City south to where the inlet juts out, till it whispers, Hey now! Ocean's blue enough! Take it to 8th and Wesley where the sidewalk says, Stand Here Let Your Shadow Tell Time. That harmonica sounds like sun on hot sidewalk, slim tapdancing shadow on concrete. Blow, till you cool it down; shiver the harp between your lips. A hum a hum. Do you know that someone loves you and wants your busy mouth, wants the reedy silver taste the player has? Oh, hummmm. Here's how you let go of love without hurting anyone: You say, "It was the music," and then you play some.

ROBERT MCDOWELL

How Does It Look to You

Listen, friend. I saw him use a Bic
To light his pipe. We'd just climbed in the car,
I looked over and poof! He'd lost his face.
That damn thing going off in a closed car
Took me back to popguns we'd packed in school,
But there he was, thirty, burning up!
We'd warned him, too, to chuck that flamethrower,
But he'd crank it up as high as it would go
And laugh at smokers jerking back their heads.
I grabbed it from him once and turned it down,
But in his hands again he wound it up.
Why? *Protection*, he would say sometimes,
Sometimes *It's a conversation starter*.
Every now and then he'd say real low
How much he hated folks with bedroom lashes.
He had them, too! But now he needn't worry.

I hit and ran red lights to Emergency
Then drove for his wife who screamed when we rushed in.
After the scream she ran. In high heels yet!
It took me a city block to reach for her,
And when I did she took a swing at me
With her purse, raising a grape on the tip of my ear.
The purse went down, and every item in it
Scattered across concrete. I had her wrists.
Then two men dropped a dolly and had me.
My arms were tied like pretzels up my back,
And something mighty heavy pressed my neck.
One guy hissed *I got him. Get police!*
I saw some shoes run off. I tried to speak,
But all I could make was a little croaking sound.
From where I lay I couldn't see high heels
But I could hear her screaming *Watch His Face!*
My mind was fuzzy by the time I heard

A squad car stop. The handcuffs bit but good.
Strong hands rolled me over, sat me up,
And sun-glare off a badge blinded me.
A voice said *After the lady's purse, creep?*
I caught my wind, laughing long and loud.
My shoulder caught a jab from a nightstick
And that shrill voice was screaming *Not His Face!*

When I could talk again I didn't laugh,
Remembering how I'd seen a joke blow up.
I stared at knees, explained the accident,
The way the victim's wife had run away
And what she'd done to me. They stood me up.
One cop behind me took away his charms
And six of us marched back to Emergency.
My friend was gone, transferred to a Burn Center,
And I thought about how much he'd laugh at me.
A doctor seconded my story.
                                        I was free.

The Workboot Boys went back to their Loading Zone;
The cops took off after making apologies.
The woman got a hypo, pawed at her nose,
And even after I thought she'd gone to sleep
Made disturbing gestures toward her face —
Like someone drowsing, waving off mosquitoes.
She muttered, too. The only words I caught
Were *No* and *Face*. Not strung together, mind,
But free-floating, striking her like bites or stings.

   Outside the sun was hot. The gutter stank.
My earlobe tingled — antiseptic wash —
My shoulder ached. I hunted up a drink
And thought of my pal and his wife.
He'd recover, work for an agency,
And do OK with low visibility.

She might learn to look at him and smile;
She might just leave a note and walk away.
I wondered what she'd dream about that night,
But I had my face to feel and think about.
I sat there drinking until the joint closed down,
Then walked on home and put my face to bed.

I counted matches striking one by one
And finally dozed around three. I wish I hadn't.
I felt her high heels stab my back and legs,
And she was chanting words I couldn't reach.
Then a pastor rolled me over, waving his hand
Above my face, and I was lifted up.
He placed her hand in mine, recited verse,
And married us right there in a Loading Zone!
We stood together, learning with every stroke
Our lips, chins, noses, cheeks, foreheads, hair.
A scar-faced crowd pressed all around us, moaning.
We shut our eyes.
                    She whispered *Honeymoon*
And we were checked in to a House of Mirrors.
In every room we entered we were new.
One morning we were three feet tall and fat;
At lunch we looked like giants with long bones;
At dinner we admired our shoulder wings.
She said *Next week we'll open the Animal Rooms.*
Who knows how long we lived there? Long enough
To learn to love variety in looks.
Distortion is the gift of second sight.
Did I say that? Did she?

Today I visited my trickster friend.
I got close to the bandages and talked.
He lay there like a matchbook on a street
But faintly squeezed my hand as I got up.
I knew just what that meant and called his wife.
We talked an hour. I asked her out to lunch.
Imagine where I'll take her after that.

JOAN McMILLAN

A Marriage Garden

When we first moved here, we thought we'd plant everything
the soil could hold, and more.
At night, we'd discuss it, intricate as a dream
or a map. The work was parceled, easy,
but you plant all day for a living, don't want to come home
and do more, I don't always have time,
all sorts of reasons lined up, a hedge,
so we discarded the idea of tulips
shining like silk hearts, the sleek slippers of iris,
blue and blue-violet, the tomatoes, carrots, and lilies.
Still, there's a peach tree
that fruits in October, despite us,
and lion-colored roses by a granite wall
above the river's poured gray glass.
I sometimes sit near its stones and moss,
my eyes on that younger couple
as they divide the ground between them like cake,
hands full of earth and water, kneeling down, digging in,
half-wild with the promise of each fertile bright life.

Overflow

Breaking through leaves, the tip of winter
spreads a fan of blood and gold
over the orchard,
this place I neglected week after week,
too late now for harvest.

Summer is pared to a husk, crumbles
to ovals of light in the grass,
small shapes I can almost pick up, hold.

August folds spokes of heat,
yields the day a child was withdrawn from my body too soon,
born in the fifth month, still hands
curled tight in death, as if around secrets

that will break the heart to discover,
splitting the hard skin
as tree bark splits at the end of a season,
cells of the green wood alive with nourishment
too sweet to be contained

like the memory of his small life
knotted to mine
overflowing this silence, drenching the roots.

DUNCAN MCNAUGHTON

Homage to Cortazar

Believe me, he said, what surrounds you, the objects, the people, the weather, the territory — none of that matters when you don't die. After you don't die you realize that all of it is nothing. You're alive in nothing. That's the medium. That's the medium you're alive in. Nothing.

Not to say being alive doesn't matter. It matters. Just that it doesn't matter in relation to anything else around you. What being alive matters to is nothing.

You see, relation ordinarily understood is a lie. Unless one breaks through that lie, then one's being alive really doesn't matter. You must not die once. Or twice. Maybe a few times. Until you get it.

Otherwise it's trivial, it's according to the lie and it doesn't matter. Instead, all the others, the people and objects and places, all of that is what matters, but your being alive doesn't. Relationally, all the people are lying. Some lie in order to lie because it pleases them to do so. Others like to suppose that they do not lie, so that's how they begin. They are all lying.

There's nothing interesting about it. It simply means that it does not matter they are alive. I.e., they think they are something.

NATHANIEL MACKEY

Song of the Andoumboulou: 13

—bedouin wind—

Back down the steps I go out
  careful not to cross my legs
    turning left up Monmouth,
                               pressing
    my feet to an otherwise all
                        but
unbearable stretch as to a lizard's back.
        In the scorched upper lefthand
      heavens my sister sits weeping,
    robed in kerosene light.
                       Our father's
  gone Panamanian grin's pathetic air,
thru which its teeth now push their deeprooting
    rotted stumps, unruly gunmetal
                      gristings,
                          a Dogon
    ram's head with Amon's gourd stuck
between its horns . . .

             Outside the
    windowless room I dance a
clubfoot's waltz, my legs driven by horsemen,
      bones hounded by lusts.
                   The last of
    eight to pierce the lighted way, my
    path readied by drumrolls, the
    oils of Amentet, the raw throats of
                     devotion . . .
Lipless thirst, our thumbless layings
  on of hands . . .

The rough body
of love at last gifted with
wings, at
last bounded on all but one
impenetrable side by the promise
of heartbeats heard on high,
wrought
promise of lips one dreamt of aimlessly
kissing,
throated rift . . . Furthered hiss of one's
gift
of tongues . . .

So this my Day, my Light's
numberless years' run of horses
whose hoofs plow any dreamer's
head, my Day of bone, my bootless
feet
mashing shattered glass, at last
begins,
white stucco walls reflect a stark summer
sun.

A distant hum the faroff buzzings of
bees, boats towed ashore . . .
The noise recedes thru every usable
gate . . .
Unruly goat, so uncorruptly
unswung,
legs rusted . . .

The risen woo the wind and
are blown
away

TOM MADEROS

The Water Plow

Life:
a bowl of rice.
The world turning over without peace.

I've seen the white walls of the woman I love
above me and beneath me,
and when we loved the waves would still collapse.

I was the one who wept for the overturned dish,
for the lie that carried the house on its back,
the awkward animal chained to a tree.

I've seen the white mills of my country grinding
and heard the voices grinding in sleep.

The grains of rice, the nations,
flooded fields in dreams—
I've seen a man pour water from a wooden pail
to his daughter's face,
shining.

The Companion

The night spreads out
its waves,
its dress,
its crude table.
The fingers of the tired man spread out,
hidden hawks that will not come to rest.

One of us counts
the stars and the lamps,
the people alive who will not sleep.

And night spreads out,
unfinished like the world.
It spills through the locks of cells,
the natural bridges.

Like leaves to wind,
it is drawn to you.

MORTON MARCUS

In 1943, the Boy Imagines That

hefty waiters swoop and whirl
among tables of roaring men,
their hands high overhead
swinging two or three bottles
by the neck, or slicing trays
through smoke like river barges
laden with merchandise.
Customers, waiters—
most wear aprons,
full-length and white,
some splattered with axle grease,
others with flour and blood.
All laugh too loudly, faces
red and sweaty, bodies
pink and hairy-black
beneath their clothes.
They shout and eat, toast
the stuffy room, yell
"To life!" and "God is good!"
eyes gleaming, fingers
snatching food from passing trays.
Those eyes know wool and grain,
plate, silver, oil and leather
in the dusty market square,
but know the people who shop there
even better; know the roads
beyond the village and where they lead.

Their cousins cry in the wilderness
and it flowers. Their uncles
rise suddenly, upsetting tables,
and dance in billowing circles
their vision of the world
that God has promised them.

And *dein mama* and *dein tochta*
scold these drunken boys,
or shriek at walls and laundry,
pots on the stove: "This can't
go on! It's not a life!"
They clasp their hands and weep,
then sigh and clean the house once more;
while in doorways on the market square,
squatting on stools, aunts and widows
tear feathers from dead hens,
and gasp each time the linen
grazes a tense nipple
inside their clothes.

          This is no country
for those who cringe and cower.
Ecstasy, reverence — yes:
these people understand
any excessive gesture,
any thought or act
that flings the leaping blood
through the body's crooked streets,
anything that grasps and grasps at life.

Laborers, shopmen, scholars,
grandmas, wives and daughters —
their every flourish and shrug,
their every toothy grin
is done in the sanctity
of God's embrace, as if the air
that encased them from head to foot,
that around them clamped
woods and fields in place,
sat on God's desk
inside a paperweight. His will was theirs,
and would be done, if they
had the patience to wait for it.

And as the boy imagines this,
his lineage, guided by gun butts,
shuffles to gas chambers
in Germany and Poland.

I Think of Those Mornings

I think of those mornings before dawn,
and it still dark out, when I'd drive
past the lighted windows of farmhouse kitchens:
first in a bus when I was ten, then on the way
to bootcamp when I was seventeen,
and now in my own car at forty-one.
There are windows still framed in my head:
the old woman in a shapeless pink dress
turning eggs or bacon in a pan;
two men I took to be bachelor brothers,
both over fifty, bald and belligerent,
seated across from each other, coffee cups
beneath their chins;
                                once, and once only,
a man and woman standing in the yellow light
holding each other by the elbows
with their fingertips;
                                but mostly
it was the woman feeding others from a fry pan
held like a lowered hand mirror at her waist;
the old man in red-and-black checkered shirt
seated alone, elbows on the table,
head tilted to catch the light, holding
an envelope or a snapshot close to his eyes.

All those lives, those and many more,
glimpsed for a moment and then gone.
Iowa, Oregon, upper New York state.
The plowed fields, corn and wheat,
breathing in the dark, a damp mist
of loam and seed.
                                Where was I headed
past those lives and never touching them,
leaving them in those farmhouses

where they rose each day before dawn
and it still dark out, switched
the light on in the kitchen, heard
not the 5:45 L.A. bus
but a truck, was it?, or a heavy-engined car
going somewhere—to Stockton, maybe,
or Portland, Denver, Duluth—
as they pulled on boots,
set plates on the table, sighed,
and watched first light, a gray light,
swim up to the window and reveal
the plowed fields, corn and wheat,
where they had left them the night before.

STEPHEN MEADOWS

Still Life: The Plain at West Point

From dozens of buses
the not yet battalions
of chaste boys
approach the stone walls
youth in those voices
glib on the wet air
coats over the shoulders
careless as heroes
the hot July rain
from far down the Hudson
thunderheads blackening the distance

a still life that moves
that day's recollection
the green plain
the bleak river valley
the boys by the hundreds
enraptured
by the great stone gate
the first of them passing
out of sight into the dark
the rest of them following
following

For My Father
Having Lost His Mind

Madrone trees knotted
above dry yellow grass
the wind down the valley
in the woods genuflecting
red limbs moving against
the hard high scope of the mountain

you sit in this thicket
speechless
amazed
your white hair disheveled
your mind a great room
where the same bit of music
strains above the sound of the wind
in the undulating branches

you hear the same music
again and again
it is the same wind you knew
half a century ago
the same sun poised
above the notch in the mountain
and the same boy waiting
in the corn
in the wind
for the night to come on
all the slow walk home
to the one light for miles
and that solace

MAUDE MEEHAN

Que Oscuras Las Sombras de Mi Sueño
How Dark the Shadows of My Dream

Small scarlet birds, swift signals of danger
scatter, become bright splashes of blood
on the worn pavement of cathedral steps.
I grope in darkness through ruins of the city.
Lean-boned children surround me, bring me rice.
A thin grey cat snakes at my ankles, waiting for kernels to drop.
I cannot eat. The little ones stand in the shadows, watching,
hold out their arms, their hands palms up, murmuring softly.
I cannot hear what they say, but I know what they ask.

At the lip of the volcano Santiago, smoke spews.
I flee from its warning, my feet bogged in ashes,
through an empty landscape where a fleshless horse stands
unprotected, unyielding, under torrential rain.
I am rescued by a Volkswagen with tin plates for armor.
There is no driver, yet I am taken quickly to the fair.
It is La Piñata, and music gives way to the voice of the Padre,
the priest poet, whose words bless the air.

I stand at the edge of the crowd. Stare into the spellbound
eyes of campesinos. They will not turn or be turned away.
The night shudders with longing. I try to speak, but my tongue
has no language. I have learned what it is that starves these
children, Nicaragua. I know now who it is.

Corcoran Lagoon
Santa Cruz, California

The breeze is pungent
with the scent of eucalyptus.
A crane perched on a floating log
preens with Edwardian elegance
oblivious to my presence.
The banks of the lagoon
are brushed with purple, pink,
pale yellow; reminders
that the seasons here
pass gently, announced by
certain flowering
or a subtle change of light.
Unlike that eastern shore
where more than fifty of my years
were weather sliced
precisely into quarters. Here
the illusion of unchanging pace
assures me there is endless time
stretched out and out. Grateful
I allow myself this small deception.

HARRYETTE MULLEN

Sugar Sandwiches

> Sugar is not a vegetable.
> — Gertrude Stein

Peaches and stomach ache. Sugar on the tongue. The daily hunger for something sweet. Sandwiches of white bread with butter and sugar. We slept like sandwiches in double-decker beds. Old army beds, painted white with surplus paint. Our beds were stacked. She'd call and we would hit the deck. Queen of diamonds, queen of hearts. The deck was stacked. Spit and polish, spick and span. We would have liked to cheat but were mostly honest in and out of Sunday school. Oh, a pack of stolen bubble gum. For which we suffered. Train up a child. Peach tree switches. The sapling bent. Our limbs were trained. We strained against our clothes, which were small and diminishing. We grew too fast, faster than the paycheck. Our clothes outstripped the budget. Therefore they were drab and useful. Our appetites were huge, though we never went hungry. We outgrew our clothes. We strained against them.

At night when they all slept I stepped out the door. I walked naked out the door into the night. Under the trees whose limbs became switches. One hand can strip off all the leaves. Remember those books you hid under your pillow? Where did you find such filth? Remember that sweater you lost? It wasn't free, you know, I had to pay for it. Where did I lose it? Where did I lose my doll, that's what I want to know. My dolls were always lost. From one house to the next. Lost in the night when we moved. Left on an airplane I only dreamed. Stolen, runover by a car. Doll heads in the street. That kind of neighborhood. Old tires and doll heads. Broken glass. Junk cars on no wheels in front yards where grass won't grow. Bare ground polished by bare feet. Boys playing in the street. Girls on curbs. Women drinking beer on porches, cutting toenails and watching cars go by. Men coming and going. Leaving something behind.

Why do they whistle at little girls and ask little boys, You get some yet? Plenty time for that. It's such a doggone shame. Now, girl, you watch yourself. I know what's out there and most of it'll ruin you if you don't know what's what. I lost my doll that I loved. She was my only baby. How could I lose her? Did I drop her in the street? Did she let go of my hand? Oh, baby, where's your mama? How could she leave you all alone? Mama's little baby, lost and alone. Who is the doll and who gets to be the girl? Who sings and who lies still? We change our clothes. We grow. Our bodies move without permission. We dance. We are the music we hear.

If someone told us we were pretty, we would laugh. Boys said, Hey, I wanna see your thang. Let me see that little kitty cat you got down there. Grown men lick their lips, say, You be ready pretty soon. Mamas say, Girl, don't be smelling your water now. It's more than a notion. Nobody to tell us, Run, laugh, dance, see how blue the sky is, daydream all you want, you got the time. She say, Stop lollygagging, fold that basket of clothes. Then you better sweep that porch like I told you.

One time we went fishing with grandpa, took off our dresses so they wouldn't get dirty. Sat on the grass in our slips, holding cane fishing poles. Didn't catch nothing. Didn't want to neither. Just sit and watch the water was enough. Summers at the swimming pool in the park. Hair gone wild. Not to have to sit for hours smelling burning hair. Not to have grease on the neck or a singed ear. Blue water and a faded bathing suit and dill pickles and peppermint sticks and going nappy all summer surrounded by troublesome boys. A couple of tenderheaded girls. Sisters. Finding pennies to spend on candy. Selling bottles to the corner store or clothes hangers to the cleaners for coins to buy sweets. Baby Ruth, Mr. Goodbar, Hershey with Almonds, Sugar Babies. Cherry Koolaid. All that sugar. Sugar sandwiches. We'd lick our plates. We'd sleep with cats. We would drink water from the same glass. We'd drink without swallowing, spitting the water back into the glass until some grown person said, Stop that! If they started to get up, we would run. We could stay gone until dinner time. Sun still shining. Long days, screen door banging. Stay in or stay out. Stop letting in all these flies.

Shorts and Pay-Less sandals. Scratching mosquito bites. I told

you to stop that! Buying a popsicle from an old bread truck —
painted over, cold inside, musical and loud. Running to catch it
after begging for a dime. Difficult to choose sometimes between
spending a dime or admiring how it looks in your hand. Sometimes
just to keep it and look at it. Like there will never be another. Except
when the music of that truck goes by. That dime barely warm in
your hand.

Watermelon trucks. The man will stop and open a jackknife to
cut you a piece for a sample. He carries a knife in his pocket. He
sings. Makes your throat itch for a red meat watermelon. If you
swallow the seeds, your stomach will stretch and vines will grow
out of your ears. We stretch our legs in the sun. Every day our
legs are longer. And we get even darker. We are black and wild.
Our hair cannot be tamed. We hide the combs until Sunday when
we must cry our tenderhead tears. Listen to a hot sermon, fan
ourselves, hoping for a breeze, hair held down. A Sunday dress
with pleats. A white collar. You try not to sweat. Cool pennies
from purse to collection plate. Not to spend on candy.

Nights when she said, Wake up, ya'll. I got a taste for some
barbecue — and we would go in our pajamas for ribs with sauce
and soft white bread. Wide awake now in the car, looking for an
open place to satisfy the craving. Riding in a truck out to the country. Preserved peaches with cloves suspended in sugar syrup. Berry
cobbler, apple butter. Black molasses. Chasing lightning bugs, streaks
of green in the heat. Hide and seek. The itch of hay. More stars.
Musical insects. The best sleep. Thick ham for breakfast. Biscuits
and butter. Eggs that might have been chickens. A country mile.
A city block. Cornbread and sweet milk. Something for our growing
bones. We grow out of our clothes. We grow faster than hard-earned
money. They say, Come give me a kiss. Give me some of that brown
sugar. A taste of something sweet. You never lose the taste for it.
We change our clothes, we keep on growing. Our bodies move
without permission. We dance. In white slips we would be ballerinas
to whom no one sends flowers. If someone told us we were pretty,
we would laugh.

SHARMAN MURPHY

Braids

I'm in between—no, more likely I'm beside—
my mother's knees. She's sitting
by the cabinet with the dishes in it.
Over the cabinet you can see the wooden
dinner bench that figures largely in a novel
I will write later, at my mother's desk, when I am nine.

Mother doesn't look right at me.
I wanted to be an ambassador, she says.
That's someone who goes to other countries
and works with their governments. But
all those people are men.

The southern California sunlight
lances through dust motes—sluices
where the fairies dance, according to my mother—
to the concrete maroon tiles of our living room floor.
At night we pretend the tiles swarm with piranha.
Only the throw-rugs and furniture are safe.

Mother's wearing her wide-leg shorts that will be in style
thirty years later. In our photograph album she is hanging
up the laundry, dressed in those shorts, her long hair
braided down her back. The caption, in her hand,
says "The Washerwoman." The picture makes
the shorts' wide checks look black and white.

She has four children, three boys and me.
My own long hair she braids each morning,
two braids, in a hurry. Each morning I cry. It hurts.

As she talks, she might take my braids
idly in her hands, but she doesn't.
I always wished I had been born a boy, she says.

TILLIE OLSEN

Dream-Vision

In the winter of 1955, in her last weeks of life, my mother—so much of whose waking life had been a nightmare, that common everyday nightmare of hardship, limitation, longing; of baffling struggle to raise six children in a world hostile to human unfolding—my mother, dying of cancer, had beautiful dream-visions—in color.

Already beyond calendar time, she could not have known that the last dream she had breath to tell came to her on Christmas Eve. Nor, conscious, would she have named it so. As a girl in long ago Czarist Russia, she had sternly broken with all observances of organized religion, associating it with pogroms and wars; "mind forg'd manacles"; a repressive state. We did not observe religious holidays in her house.

Perhaps, in her last consciousness, she *did* know that the year was drawing towards that solstice time of the shortest light, the longest dark, the cruellest cold, when—as she had explained to us as children—poorly sheltered ancient peoples in northern climes had summoned their resources to make out of song, light, food, expressions of human love—festivals of courage, hope, warmth, belief.

It seemed to her that there was a knocking at her door. Even as she rose to open it, she guessed who would be there, for she heard the neighing of camels. (I did not say to her: "Ma, camels don't neigh.") Against the frosty lights of a far city she had never seen, "a city holy to three faiths," she said, the three wise men stood: magnificent in jewelled robes of crimson, of gold, of royal blue.

"Have you lost your way?" she asked. "Else, why do you come to me? I am not religious, I am not a believer."

"To talk with *you*, we came," the wise man whose skin was black and robe crimson, assured her, "to talk of whys, of wisdom."

"Come in then, come in and be warm—and welcome. I have

starved for such talk."

But as they began to talk, she saw that they were not men, but women:

That they were not dressed in jewelled robes, but in the coarse every-day shifts and shawls of the old country women of her childhood, their feet wrapped round and round with rags for lack of boots; snow now sifting into the room;

That their speech was not highflown, but homilies; their bodies not lordly in bearing, magnificent, but stunted, misshapen — used all their lives as a beast of burden is used;

That the camels were not camels, but farm beasts, such as were kept in the house all winter, their white cow breaths steaming into the cold.

And now it was many women, a babble.

One old woman, seamed and bent, began to sing. Swaying, the others joined her, their faces and voices transfiguring as they sang; my mother, through cracked lips, singing too — a lullaby.

For in the shining cloud of their breaths, a baby lay, breathing the universal sounds every human baby makes, sounds out of which are made all the separate languages of the world.

Singing, one by one the women cradled and sheltered the baby.

"The joy, the reason to believe," my mother said, "the hope for the world, the baby, holy with possibility, that is all of us at birth." And she began to cry, out of the dream and its telling now.

"Still I feel the baby in my arms, the human baby," crying now so I could scarcely make out the words, "the human baby, before we are misshapen; crucified into a sex, a color, a walk of life, a nationality . . . and the world yet warrings and winter."

I had seen my mother but three times in my adult life, separated as we were by the continent between, by lack of means, by jobs I had to keep and by the needs of my four children. She could scarcely write English — her only education in this country a few months of night school. What at last I flew to her, it was in the last days she had language at all. Too late to talk with her of what was in our hearts; or of harms and crucifying and strengths as she had known and experienced them; or of whys and knowledge, of wisdom. She died a few weeks later.

She, who had no wordly goods to leave, yet left to me an inexhaustible legacy. Inherent in it, this heritage of summoning resources to make — out of song, food, warmth, expressions of human love — courage, hope, resistance, belief; this vision of universality, before the lessenings, harms, divisions of the world are visited upon it.

She sheltered and carried that belief, that wisdom — as she sheltered and carried us, and others — throughout a lifetime lived in a world whose season was, as still it is, a time of winter.

SHERRI PARIS

Two Women

> Two women sleeping together
> have more than their sleep to defend.
> — *Adrienne Rich*

I. We come to the sea, after the floods have passed.
    Debris, mudwrecked homes,
    the broken bones of our city
    lay in the roads.
    Foundations have washed away,
    and many wander like refugees
    at the breast of the awful tide.

II. You and I have come here together
    new.
    With no language between us,
    no definitions for what we are.
    The words we learned in our father's homes
    are exhausted.
    You stare into the tide pools.
    Your eyes a blue
    the sea only dreams of,
    reveals only to painters and poets
    who crave romance
    who use the words we deny
    the words which deny us.
    I lay beside you in the sand
    still and alert
    like a reptile.
    On your knees,
    you separate
    the many winding strands of my hair,
    while anemones wave their arms
    very slowly
    like children yawning.
    "Each pool," you say,
    "is ecologically perfect. A balanced world."

III. Two women on a beach are strangers
     to others passing
     to ourselves.
     We stand with the rocks
     beaten
     by waters
     which once gave birth
     and now take it back slowly.
     A broken bottle neck floats by
     with no note inside to explain us,
     as I hold your stranger's body
     so like my own
     as if I could re-create you
     as if I could re-member a woman
     who never learned that beauty hurts
     never starved herself
     nor bound her breasts
     nor stopped her blood from flowing freely
     never learned the foreign language
     of history.
     I touch your face
     to soothe the lines
     of stress and exhaustion
     to print your cheeks instead
     with the lines of my palm
     merging our destinies
     mundane yet esoteric.
     "When I was pregnant," you say,
     "I laid on this sand
     and opened my legs to the tides
     feeling this terrible pull
     as my child moved with the sea."
     At such moments, we may want
     one another,
     but the tide recedes inevitably
     leaving only great distances.

IV. Later,
         we walk arm-in-arm by the water
         which has washed the land.
         The trees mourn on the edges
         of bleached sands
         raising their broken arms
         like amputees
         who suffer what is absent.

DALE PENDELL

Myrtle Street

The men who built this house walked to work,
    or rode horses;
They built with dimension lumber, delivered by wagon;
    Hihn's sawmill had just replaced oxen with steam.

They were good with wood, careful of nails,
    and wore hats if they weren't in bed.
They probably helped frame the big casino, downtown.
The street was here, just as wide, but unpaved.
    A lot of work had already been done: city water,
Electricity, sewer, telephone. They cracked
    crude oil for water gas.

The perimeter is made of large round riverstones,
    lifted by hand and pulled here in a buckboard.
It looks like they mixed the cement a little at a time,
    in wheelbarrows. Digging near their foundation,
I struck an old, thick-rimmed glass milk bottle;
    all the ice came from the Sierras, in sawdust.

It was a time of fast changes: Albert Einstein
    not yet published, Pound and Williams still in school.
A hundred years before the house was started, Indians
    at the Mission revolted and killed the priest.
Before the house needed repainting, the county's
    redwoods were stumped and the mills shut.

1904/1984

VICTOR PERERA

A Show of Strength

One morning a picture of Coco Montcrassi appeared on the front page of *El Imparcial*. This was two months after the overthrow of the dictator, Jorge Ubico, and six months before democratic elections. Coco was in cub scout (*aguilete*) uniform, with one hand raised imperiously to an approaching car. The caption under the picture read: "Young patriot enjoys reward of service to his country in its hour of need."

I dug out my *aguilete* outfit from the family discard-trunk and rushed outside to direct traffic. By the time Father came home at midday and scolded me for not asking his permission I had finessed across our intersection one ox-cart, five automobiles, a dozen motorcycles, forty to fifty bicycles, and countless pedestrians. One of the motorists had stopped to pat my head and deposit five centavos in my talented palm.

The next day was Sunday, and I quit early and wandered to Coco's post on Sexta Avenida and Thirteenth, just outside his father's sausage plant.

"I have been appointed Assistant Chief of Traffic Directors for this district," Coco called out, lofty and cool under his striped umbrella.

"Felicitations," I said, not the least surprised. I always knew Coco would go far. My eyes bulged, however, when he showed me his week's haul from public-spirited motorists: one police whistle, a tarnished police shield, a fistful of coins and bills amounting to three quetzales.

"That's very good," I said, adding with calculated understatement, "Where I am . . . I don't even have an umbrella."

"This is nothing," Coco said. "Tomorrow I'll be moved to Eleventh Street, across from the Lux Theater. There I'll really clean up."

I whistled. "Your parents won't object?" The Lux intersection was rife with commotion.

"My parents grant me absolute autonomy," said Coco, parroting one of the slogans of the day.

Coco blew his whistle and signaled a right turn to a Buick sedan. Into Coco's extended right palm the driver of the Buick dropped, as he slowed for the turn, a large silver coin. Coco closed his hand and pocketed the emolument like a professional. "If you want," he said, twirling his whistle, "I can arrange with the chief traffic director to assign you this post."

"No thanks," I said, dejected. "Father wouldn't allow it. It's too far from home."

Coco gazed down from his shaded platform, and raised an eyebrow. "*Must* he know?"

"He'd find out. One of the salesgirls is sure to pass this way and see me." My gloom deepened.

"That is a shame," Coco said, "because—" He stopped midsentence to signal a left-turning Harley-Davidson. "It is a shame, I say, because I had a proposition to make to you."

"Oh? What kind?" I was wary.

"I was going to propose you join me on the scout march next Sunday."

"What scout march?"

"Don't you read the papers?" From his back pocket Coco drew a folded copy of *El Imparcial* and opened it to a full-page announcement in the center:

Attention All Scouts: There is to be held a full-dress march through the streets of our Capital on Sunday March 11, 1945. All Scouts are to assemble in full uniform on the southeast corner of Parque Central by six-thirty a.m. Your participation in this extraordinary event, in view of the present crisis of our Republic, is vital and mandatory.

Your Scoutmaster,
Robert Urrutia, Lic. D.D.

"What is the march for?" I asked.

"What do you think? Use your head." He tapped his left temple.

"A *manifestación?*"

"Precisely. It is a show of strength to give criminal elements the impression that public order has been restored."

"I see."

"It is an obvious ruse, of course, but it has its merits. And it might work."

I read the notice again. "But this doesn't mention cubs. It doesn't say *Aguiletes* are included."

Coco sighed. "Look again. It says 'All Scouts' at the top."

"True," I conceded.

"'All Scouts' means *All* Scouts, which categorically and by definition includes *Aguilas* and *Aguiletes.*"

I said nothing. One does not lightly contradict a logician of Coco's caliber.

"Examine the evidence carefully," said Coco, signaling to a cyclist, "You will understand my conclusion."

"Granted," I said, "but it's out of the question. My father would give me hell." I did not mention that I was no longer a dues-paying member of the force. I had quit the previous year after fainting twice on an expedition to the top of Pacaya Volcano.

Again Coco gazed down and raised an eyebrow. This time I guessed his drift.

We agreed to meet in Parque Central at six-fifteen A.M. To forestall the embarrassment of a parental veto we decided not to seek their permission.

I rose at dawn next Sunday, tiptoed to the laundry room and slipped on my *aguilete* uniform: short olive trousers and shirt, red scarf, olive cap. The first wisps of color had stained the eastern sky when I got to the park, where a dozen scouts had already assembled, tall, lean, consciously adult in long trousers. I sat down to await Coco on a tile bench, my teeth chattering from the cold. After fifteen minutes more scouts arrived and milled about, but there was no sign of Coco. The icy tiles raised goose flesh on my scrotum. I wondered desolately if Coco had been found out or had overslept.

By six-thirty I felt betrayed. I was debating whether to stay on my cold bench, or creep home through the labyrinth, when I heard a familiar voice from the crowd.

"Ey, short-pants, are you marching today?"

"Could be," I said, sitting up. I attached the taunt and its matching sneer to the pimply face of an I.S. sixth-grader, a notorious rowdy named Ortíz.

"Well, you will have to march by yourself then. You're too tall for the rest of us."

"Could be," I said, rising stiffly.

The scoutmaster blew his whistle and the scouts fell into ranks of three. With Ortíz's remark still rankling I marched to the end of the column and formed an orderly rank of one.

The scoutmaster approached me, his whistle clamped between his teeth.

"Your name?"

"Nissen, sir, Jaime. At your service."

"Rank?"

"*Aguilete*, sir. Eastern district."

He twirled the whistle between thumb and forefinger. "H'm. I don't recall seeing you at the lodge." He said this weightily, as if he were about to unmask a cunning saboteur. "Are you in Cazeras's troop?"

"Yes, sir." I had, in fact, been in Cazeras's troop. But that was before the ill-fated expedition to Pacaya Volcano.

"But this march is for *aguilas.*"

"With your permission, Don Roberto, the notice in the paper read 'All Scouts,' which categorically and by definition includes *aguiletes*, if you please, sir."

"All right. But you will have to stay abreast of the platoon. Keep in mind, this is a serious march, not a parade. Do not expect to be nursed."

"Yes, sir — no, sir."

"The decision is yours." He backed away and made another count of his troops. I was still the odd number.

The whistle blew. Don Roberto shouted, *"De frente . . . márchen."* The drummer struck up the roll and we started with a brisk stamp and step toward the mouth of Sexta Avenida.

"*Un . . . dos . . . un . . . dos . . . un . . . dos . . .*" Don Roberto barked the count with military precision. All the legs in step: a brushing tattoo against the pavement, stiff arms swinging in a smooth, even rhythm. And the drum — "plam . . . terraplam" — to provide the proper martial spirit.

We turned into Sexta Avenida in perfect stride, a single flawless engine. At once I heard the deferential murmur from spectators lining the streets. A rising swell lifted me up and carried me on its back. This was the moment I'd been waiting for since I was five years old.

We passed Father's store and the murmurs from the crowds turned to cheers. Coco had been right. This was a show of strength, a demonstration that sanity and public order had been restored.

On the polished fender of a parked automobile the tops of buildings flowed past, like the panorama in a newsreel. . . . I snapped my straying eyes back to the precise midpoint between shoulder blades of the scout ahead of me.

As we approached the Lux Theater the cheers and exclamations rose in a single voice. The entire city had turned out to greet us! At long last the months of anarchy and bloodshed were at an end. . . . Poor Coco, I felt no rancor toward him now, fast asleep in his coward's bed. I pitied him for missing this experience of patriotism — *real* patriotism. For the first time I felt at one with my country of birth, my homeland, Guatemala. Long live the Revolution!

The tops of buildings vanished from my fixed line of vision. We were in the marketplace, and the cheers from the crowds grew so loud I lost count and fell out of step. At the same time an irresistible curiosity overcame me. I turned my head slightly and strained my eyes to the right. Then I strained them to the left. They met with two solid walls of mocking faces and convulsed bodies. I looked again, in disbelief. There was no mistake. The cheers had turned to raucous jeers and hoots. The target of these jeers, and of dozens of pointing arms, was me. When I looked back I had fallen several paces behind. I realized all at once the spectacle I presented: knee-length trousers, spindly legs, the shortest in the squad by a head; and all of it lagging three yards behind in a now thoroughly demoralized rank of one.

I tried to skip back into step, but my heart was no longer in it. The illusion of oneness had been shattered. I was no longer a soldier but a straggler, laboring hopelessly to stay abreast of his betters.

Gales of laughter swept the length of the avenue. We were in the slums beyond the Barrio Chino, where the city's poor and the squatters live. Behind us a band of urchins burlesqued our stride, sniggering obscenely. An object whizzed past my ear and struck the scout ahead of me. On the packed sidewalks the mood turned festive. Men and women danced and clapped their hands to invisible marimbas. Fathers hoisted giggling infants to their shoulders for a better view. Mothers vanished behind grille windows to fetch their children and were replaced by grandfathers with toothless grins. More objects whizzed by and rolled along the pavement. Shoe-polish tins!

An urchin tugged at the seat of my trousers as the crowd egged him on. I was six paces behind now and dog-trotting with a hand on my cap to keep from falling farther back. The urchins began to pester the scouts up front, like a swarm of locusts. The scoutmaster ordered a jog-step—needlessly in my case, I was in full canter. An urchin leaped for Don Roberto's scarf, to the approving roar of the crowds. When a flying tin hit a scout on the head, Don Roberto blew his whistle and outran his troops to shelter inside the railway station.

I could not get away for I was engulfed by a half-dozen squealing imps bent on tearing off my clothes. I flailed and kicked at them but they made off with my cap, scarf, belt, and the back of my shirt. Stripped of my last vestiges of dignity I dodged into the railway urinal and waited, crouched against the wall, for the crowds to disperse.

I made my way home along the city's back streets. When I arrived, half-naked and in tears, my parents and Coco were waiting in the hallway. Mother broke down when she saw me, and Father's gray face made it clear there would be no harsh reprimands; nor would it have mattered much if there were.

Afterward I demanded an explanation from Coco.

"Father," he said. "He caught me sneaking out the back."

I studied his face. There was no condescension in it now, nor the smug self-assurance. It was an eleven-year-old's face, very pale and on the verge of tears. Then I saw the telltale smudge on his lip.

"What is that on your lip?"

"Ice cream. Chocolate."

"You lied about your father."

"Yes. I had second thoughts last night, but it was too late to call you."

"Dirty coward." I gave him a shove.

"I am not," he said, and shoved me back. "I would have called you."

"Dirty Frenchy coward." I shoved him again.

We grappled and fell to the ground, rolling over and over, pummeling each other's sides.

"It was horrible," I said, pressing my knuckles to his throat.

"I know, I know," he gasped. "We heard on the radio."

We wrestled and rolled all over the floor, sobbing, no longer pummeling but clinging to one another in a tight embrace.

ROBERT PETERSON

Baseball

In the last pocket of a threadbare afternoon
I found a park some boys,
five on one side
seven on the other,
were having Baseball
homeplate on a hill,
firstbase an imaginary place
everyone knew where was,
and out beyond
a real pond ducks sailed on.

The sides called
Come on and play Ump
and catcher-for-bothsides,
So I came on and we had
Baseball
for a long long time
until nobody remembered the score,
until we were only Three
against Two, six
shadows tilting under one evening star. . . .

Calling Muzi (1971 – 1986)

For most of our years, Mooska, I kept you in, away from wars
    & cars.
"Cat-going-up-a-mountain," an Indian named you. Now, so you've
        gone wild, & done.

In this window you watched the neighbor's dog laze, &
    hummingbirds
        shimmer in fuchsia.
Here you dreamed of Taos; I'd rap your nose through the glass
        & make a face.

Table you warmed, claw you honed, wisp of fur.
The comb, the talk, the whisker, the legs, the play; a late flea,
        water dish, still; empty box, that silver gaze.

Where will your shy spirit, my doe, be happy to linger now?
In your final hour, by the lighthouse, long stem of pelicans
        trembling west, *legato*.

"To be truly alive, a man should always wear a cat on his head."
Last notes of a nocturne, for your quiet, gentle ways.

BERNICE RENDRICK

Grandmother's Onion Sandwiches

You showed me spring
as we walked the length of your backyard.
We paused at the honeysuckle vine,
passed the smokehouse,
the crabapple tree
to the stretch of Kansas earth
where you let go of my hand
and bowed down
to pull the season's first green onions.
I smelled what spring was,
the sweet rising of roots
and decaying leaves, the mud puddles
all warming in the sun.
On the way back
you stopped at the pump to rinse
dirt from the sleek scallions.
In the kitchen you sliced them
on buttered bread, pried open
the last of winter's applesauce.

The next day I went there alone.
You found me yanking
more of the sweet spring bulbs,
eating them dirt and all.
Not knowing yet
what was what—
but knowing the smell, the taste
were buried there.
Knowing I wanted more.

A Long Walk Through Snow

You are six again, outgrowing
your sister's brown oxfords,
the perpetual blisters
gluing skin to your stockings.
Your mangled feet are healed,
now shod in soft leather
but still you limp
from the lessons of those years.

Your sister and you walk two miles
to school, swing tin lunchpails,
open them to potted meat sandwiches,
cookies, if there are any.
You scuff along, puffing
your breath like cigarette smoke,
toss stones at the grey slush
in the stubbled fields

snowflakes fall over the acres
your father plants with wheat,
fall on the land your Mother detests.
A soft white sheet drapes
the lost hope of the oilwell,
glazes the fenceposts
that guide you home in storms.

Turning into the windy second mile
of what you're taught
was once a shallow sea, you recite
Books of the Bible for Sunday's stars:
Genesis, Exodus, Leviticus, Numbers. . . .
then shout the Lord's prayer
into the cold, omnipresent air.

ADRIENNE RICH

Blue Rock

for Myriam Díaz-Diocaretz

Your chunk of lapis-lazuli shoots its stain
blue into the wineglass on the table

the full moon moving up the sky is plain
as the dead rose and the live buds on one stem

No, this isn't Persian poetry I'm quoting:
all this is here in North America

where I sit trying to kindle fire
from what's already on fire:

the light of a blue rock from Chile swimming
in the apricot liquid called "eye of the swan".

This is a chunk of your world, a piece of its heart:
split from the rest, does it suffer?

You needn't tell me. Sometimes I hear it singing
by the waters of Babylon, in a strange land

sometimes it just lies heavy in my hand
with the heaviness of silent seismic knowledge

a blue rock in a foreign land, an exile
excised but never separated

from the gashed heart, its mountains,
winter rains, language, native sorrow.

At the end of the twentieth century
cardiac graphs of torture reply to poetry

line by line: in North America
the strokes of the stylus continue

the figures of terror are reinvented
all night, after I turn the lamp off, blotting

wineglass, rock and roses, leaving pages
like this scrawled with mistakes and love,

falling asleep; but the stylus does not sleep,
cruelly the drum revolves, cruelty writes its name.

Once when I wrote poems they did not change
left overnight on the page

they stayed as they were and daylight broke
on the lines, as on the clotheslines in the yard

heavy with clothes forgotten or left out
for a better sun next day

But now I know what happens while I sleep
and when I wake the poem has changed:

the facts have dilated it, or cancelled it;
and in every morning's light, your rock is there.

GAËL ROZIÈRE

Monterey Bay

Where redwood silhouettes
        bend in sanctum
Santa Cruz emerges from hills
        then juts out
to the cold sonorous ocean
        Behind
the bay opens extended
        scarcely touched
till the cypresses of Carmel like nuns' arms
        reclaim it
The moon
        lies on its side
                        like a harlequin
        Fog drifts over the rippled water
Far away mountains
        stand as a border
                And I think of Rio
                        Acapulco
                    Samana
At night the sky is deep
        and blue enough
to remind you of the Equator
        so that the stars seem
ready to drop into your mouth
        like clams
or mangoes

Kyle at Thirteen Months

You toddle across the meadow in your first pair of shoes
open and close your fingers in bye-bye motion.
I wave back as you move away on legs
dimpled and firm, your eyes
on the pebbles to be grabbed,
the yellow flowers ahead.
Before I can fully breathe
you are a speck in the distance
and I the heart in each blade of grass around you.

PRISCILLA W. SHAW

Rip Tide

When it finally happened
time became double, she was both
in her body and outside it.
She could watch from above the tiny
figure moving in the ocean,
breast stroke almost a dog paddle
nose pointed, hands that worked.
But inside/below she was slowly
losing ground/her motions grew stronger
but she wasn't advancing on
the buildings that her eyes
sighted on shore and held fast,
her body slipped despite her
silent inside wet water noise
drifting backward as
fear crossed over into
trance
lulled itself
in a dream swimming nowhere.

The extreme cold of the water
continually surprised the rest of her
waiting at the edges
to draw her heat out
steal all the warmth.

The idea of it actually the chief whack
in the groin, fear that the
searing ice heat would
collapse back
betrayed by thought

and there would come a coldness
walls caving in
the warm pocket of her body
flooded then with foreignness
membranes permeated and gone.

Between her and the shore rose steep mountains
of slick hurrying water rearing
to crash down
enter the danger zone
and be grasped, vertigo of a building
toppling onto her two three times higher
than herself, her person scrambled
and struggling inside the whirling
sand and water cavern, funnel
to suck her or toss her, siphon her
into the barnacle-lined piles
of the nearby wharf.

The hard hazy sun was still
shining and a few ordinary off-season
people scattered about the
beach were talking almost within reach.
In a voice out of a tea party
she heard herself saying distinctly
but polite as if asking a favor
—Could you possibly help me?—
and a young man she didn't know
answering—What?—so she had to say again,
her politeness more urgent
—Could you HELP me?—
Now sure he had heard
he started forward in the water
holding out his hand and thrusting it
till it reached her somehow and pulled her
toward shore, company through the water while

she swam too, not at all like a rescue,
as if they were old friends
rushing toward each other and meeting
in a busy place.

Then it was all over and there they were
in a small group chatting noisily:
the safe bit of excitement had
brushed them all and they could feel it
in their skin feathers, rapidly telling
one another everything about rip
tides they had known.

TIMOTHY SHEEHAN

Snowfall

Outside our tent
geese have been landing
since before dawn,
landing in this first snowfall
which has lasted all night.
Already many are dead,
feathers crusting with snow,
and in their confusion
others are squalling
in the white chaparral.

I drop the flap of the tent
and try to wake you.
But you turn from me
still sleeping,
and your hair falls over the ground
where, inches away, a bird
works its head under the canvas
into our tent,
the bill snapping,
dark eyes beginning to freeze.

Tuis Ka

In Mayan the word for full moon and onion is the same,
so when by chance the moon is unearthed and served with dinner
that evening, or an onion rises above the horizon on a clear night
there is no harm, only the onion lighting the lettuce leaf on
    the tongue
only the odor of the moon making coyotes howl and weep.

MARJORIE SIMON

Eve

When the moon silvers
           sleep
you understand
the hardness of an oyster's tears how
its soul weeps pearls
           the shadow
remains on the wall
when the room is empty
           the dream
that escapes from its chains
and returns to be forgotten
empty suitcase by the door
mirror in search of
           the face
inside your window

All those other heartbeats
can not cover my
           silence
and from the hollow
of your rib where
nothing else grows
my name
           indelible

PHILLIP SLATER

In Which I Get Very Little Help from My Friends

In a way my adventures began right after I got out of the hospital, when I went to a film about nuclear war. It wasn't my idea of a welcome-home party. I would have preferred seeing something nostalgic with Carole Lombard or Sydney Greenstreet at the theater where all the film buffs go: Young men with bulging glasses who twirl their hair between their fingers when they talk. But I don't like going to the movies alone and I didn't think sitting in a dark room with a lot of people twirling their hair would be good for me right then.

So I went to this nuclear film at the local community center with my friends Peter and Grace who are very political. They said they wanted to celebrate my return to normality by making me realize we were all in the same boat. The image made me recoil a little — boats full of people and all — but I went anyway because I wanted company.

The film was very disturbing. There were pictures of Hiroshima after the bomb fell, shots of hospital wards full of radiation victims, and speeches by some men who used to be mad scientists. Grace claims there's an organization called Scientists Anonymous where repentant scientists get together at night and smoke a lot of cigarettes and tell each other how they used to spend weeks at a time prowling around their laboratories — going without food, sleeping on the floor, letting their personal appearance deteriorate, destroying their bodies and their marriages. They especially like to testify that in the depth of their illness they would have murdered their loved ones for a Nobel Prize. And if a member is caught writing formulas on his sleeve they throw him right out of the meeting. At least that's what Grace says.

After the film a folksinger came on with a guitar and sang a little song about nuclear war:

Nuclear war
S'like wood alcohol
Gonna make you blind
Gonna kill y'all.

And then there was a discussion.

Everybody wanted to know what they could do. The woman who showed the film said that really everyone should do what they can do best. Which didn't help me much because the only thing I'm really superior at is cat's cradle and I couldn't see how that would help. Peter and Grace decided to do some organizing, but I said that wouldn't do for me since I can't even organize my own life. Grace said that didn't matter—that that's why people *did* organizing. I said that meeting new people right now would throw me into a funk. She said I had to start somewhere. I said you have to start at the beginning and not at the end, and she dropped it. It's one of the few arguments I've ever won with Grace.

I think I'm beginning to understand how Grace's mind works. At the meeting she was quite short with some people she called "trout radicals." She said they like to spend their time swimming upstream so they can have the security of staying in the same place and still retain the illusion of movement. Or something like that. She said you have to use the energy of the stream itself to change its direction, but she didn't say how to go about it. Grace studies some kind of martial art and it influences the way she thinks about life.

It was Grace who suggested I write a letter. We were sitting at the Caffé Salieri late one afternoon a few days later and she was bored with me asking what I should do. Peter, grumbling behind his *Guardian*, said that any fool could write letters.

"Never mind," Grace said. "I'm trying to appeal to Taylor's modesty."

It was a delicate way to put it and she was right. It might be a dumb, pointless thing to do, but I wasn't feeling all that confident right then, and for someone just discharged from a mental hospital a small manageable task was very welcome.

I thought about it as we left the Salieri and rode up in the hills above Las Lunas to watch the sunset. Las Lunas, I suppose, is everyone's fantasy of what a laid-back coastal California town should be like. It has a population of about seventy thousand, a university, an electronics firm, a lot of fruit trees and artichokes, a Native American burial ground, and tourists. It has, per capita, more astrologers, real estate agents, chiropractors, espresso bars, movie theaters, and tarot decks than any place in America. It also has more unemployed artists, musicians, writers, craftspeople, actors, poets, dancers, and carpenters, and the only free soup kitchen I know of where there are two lines — one for vegetarians.

We drove up in Grace's 1969 Pontiac convertible, which Peter likes to call the Coupe de Grace. I brought some bread and Grace brought a bottle of red wine and some Brie. Peter brought some macadamia nuts, but he only let us have three apiece because he wanted to save them for the woman he was meeting later.

"These," he said, holding up the jar, "have unlocked many an armored heart."

"No woman who invites you to come for dinner and spend the night qualifies as an 'armored heart,' " Grace objected. "Cough up."

So Peter relented and gave us two more each.

"Look at those colors, Taylor!" Grace loved sunsets. "Think how lucky we are to be living in an age of decline!"

Which was a pretty thin piece of encouragement, but better than nothing.

When I got home that night I started right away trying to compose my letter to the Pentagon. It was harder than I thought. I had all the arguments in front of me but I didn't know what order to put them in. I got more and more discouraged, and after a while I found myself staring at a little seven-legged spider in a web between the TV and the wall — anything to avoid looking at that blank page with "Dear Sir" at the top. The spider kept trying to wrap a dying fly up for storage but every time she finished, it would sneak off and unravel itself. Then it would try to fly, but could only manage to heave itself out of the web and onto the floor beside the TV. The spider would then have to scuttle down and carry it up again—giving it a few more injections to keep it quiet—and the process would start all over.

I remembered the story of Robert de Bruce, the liberator of Scotland, who was heartened in a dark moment by the perseverance of a spider. Was this messy drama meant for me? Did it mean I should keep trying? Is a busy spider always an advertisement for perseverance? When I told Grace about it the next day she suggested that maybe the message was being conveyed by the fly, but fortunately I didn't think of that at the time. Because after watching the spider for an hour or so I found myself writing a passionate letter to the secretary of defense, which I finished in twenty minutes and mailed the next day without making a single alteration.

This incident was the beginning of a long and complex relationship between the spider and me. When I got home the next night, pleased with having achieved my modest goal, I looked for her again. She was building a web and still having trouble. Every time she started out with a new strand she'd see her reflection in the blank screen of the TV, get disoriented, and go back the way she came. Her whole web was just a mass of loops that dangled uselessly from her point of origin. I began to wonder about her. Was this the same species that had inspired Robert de Bruce? Had it been wise to seek inspiration from a creature too stupid to navigate across its own web? But the die was cast.

A few weeks later I received a reply to my letter.

Dear Mr. Bishop:

Thank you for your letter setting out the dangers of nuclear escalation. We here at the Pentagon are very much alive to the perils you have so eloquently described. We appreciate your concern, your anxiety, your sincere desire to dissuade our nation from a course that seems, as you put it, suicidal. But how do you think we feel? Shut up in a huge impersonal office all day with a noisy air conditioner, answering letters from people who think they know more than the Department of Defense. You talk about destroying the world—what about unemployment? I have a family to support just like you.

You claim that the USSR is more cautious than we are just because they lost twenty million people in World War II. But how many people in Russia remember that stuff? Our thinking on this at DOD is a little more sophisticated. We take into account not only memory but also imagination, in which we've got them beat hands down. Could a Russian have invented the electric can opener or liquid rust arrester? A few old Stalinists may remember the German invasion, but here we have a nation full of imaginative people visualizing a world gone mad with nuclear warheads flying about as thick as midges in a summer swamp and reducing the planet to a smoking, lifeless cinder. Remember, the Russians only think what they're told, whereas Americans think for themselves. And in case there are some Americans who do think what they're told, we tell them as little as possible, just to be on the safe side.

You claim that we already have a larger nuclear arsenal than the Soviets, but this is not an easy thing to assess. There are many different types of warheads, many different kinds of delivery systems, and many different ways to defend against them. So you can see, Mr. Bishop, it isn't a simple matter. Perhaps I can illustrate the problem by drawing a little analogy:

Standing alone, before a mirror, a man might look at his penis and feel that it was quite handsome and more than adequate to do the job required of it. But let that same man stroll through a locker room and you'll see his attitude change. He compares himself with others, and begins to be aware of certain limitations. His may be of unusual length, but the man next to him will boast a greater thickness. He will naturally feel uneasy about this and at a disadvantage, and so will the other man. I hope this will make clear to you the nature of the problem we're dealing with. We must strive at all times to be both longer and thicker than our enemies. If you have further queries, please don't hesitate to write us here at DOD.

Sincerely yours,
Lt. Col. Richard Mobey

The next day at the Salieri I showed the letter to Grace and Peter. Grace made a face.

"It's what I've always said: You'll never make a dent in this system until you get rid of all those necrophiliac political leaders. They've let their right brains atrophy so they're all lopsided. That's why they carry briefcases around all the time—to balance them. More weight on the light side, otherwise they'd fall over. In the old days they used holsters the same—"

Peter interrupted.

"I've just had a brilliant idea!" He paused for effect. "Right now both nations try to build up bigger defenses so that when they agree to disarm they'll have further to go. Right? The idea seems to be that if I throw away one missile, and then you throw away one missile, and then I do, and then you do, if I've been smart I end up with one and you end up with none. Then I can push you around. The problem is, nobody's dumb enough to be caught short. Obviously if you want to have a balance of power it's better to have more missiles than less, because it's easier to think you're equal. But you can't keep building more because it wrecks everybody's economy. So here's my plan: Barter!"

"Barter?"

"Instead of throwing the stuff away, you *trade*. I give you one of my missiles, you give me one of yours. When we've traded them all away we just trade them all back again. Then we never have to build any more. We're balanced and we're in a continual state of disarmament, yet at the same time we're building up our defenses!"

"It's inspired, Peter," Grace declared unenthusiastically, "but it doesn't go to the heart of the matter, which is that world leaders are all power-hungry to begin with or they wouldn't be where they are, and they can't be expected to make peace because they're all too driven and competitive and paranoid. We need to find ways for heads of state to fight and compete and play chicken with each other without endangering the rest of us. In the Middle Ages they had jousts and tournaments and spent their energy smashing each other up, so the peasants could go about their business and keep the world alive. . . . What is it, sweetheart?" (This to her daughter, Athene, who had been playing dolls with a friend on the other side of the

Caffé veranda but was now pulling on her arm.)

"Linda says her mother's a *bicycle!*" Athene's five-year-old treble dripped with scorn.

"She means 'bisexual,' darling. Put your sweater on, it's getting cool."

Athene grumbled herself into her sweater and ran off, as Grace completed her thought: "What we need is the functional equivalent of a joust."

Peter suggested demolition derbies in helicopters over Greenland, but he thought some sort of prize would be needed. Grace said the most appealing prize for power-hungry men would be a woman who was completely accepting and nonthreatening, i.e., recently deceased.

After another round of cappuccinos the forces of evil were reeling and Peter and Grace were ready to call it a day. But I couldn't share in their enthusiasm. Their sardonic fantasies depressed me. I needed something to hold on to. Writing my own letter had made me feel a little better for a while and now I'd lost even that harmless illusion. When I got home I just sat for a long time staring at the blank screen of the unplugged TV and scratching my right eyebrow. (I have a chronic itch there. Grace says it comes from a repressed desire to be supercilious.) I hadn't moved for nearly an hour when I saw something that changed my life irrevocably.

ROZ SPAFFORD

Hibakusha

One felt ill, stayed home from classes
Another was at her sister's house
and thus lived to tell

These accidents, now
legends

Had your grandmother gone to work that day
none of us would be here
Still she cries in her sleep
and awake
when they see her scar

We know about those accidents:

If we had called her before
I should have hidden his
Someone should have called the

The last things we did, said, thought
etched into us
epitaphs

Every day a web of circumstance:

The building you are in
is it reinforced?
Do you have a short-sleeved shirt on?
How many miles are you
from

We greet
the ghosts of ourselves
blind and hairless
dripping skin
our constant white shadows

They wish we had insisted,
said, "It all stops until this does."
We could have done that

They are our new ancestors

Because of the children. Always
something. A temperature. Nightmares
about school. Not enough
time.

Because we were busy
with the dioxin in our yard
or with a job spraying dioxin
or cleaning it up,
with any job: playing pick-up sticks
every day
every day losing.

Or with trying to be loved
we were busy

They were busy
in Hiroshima

                    (*Hibakusha* is the Japanese word for
                    those who experienced the bomb.)

CAROL STAUDACHER

This Morning, Married, You Sang Again

for Susan

The orchard whines in the wind its loss of fruit.
The lone crow taunts the sky; seals bark
on their scaly miserable island, and I
lower myself against a west coast cliff, maneuver
into the sand until it molds to my body.

Singing—that is how I think of you,
singing into the kitchen to shake me loose
from a mother's small paralysis of heart,
motioning me to join you for the chorus.
Or singing away your occasional fear
straining your voice to comical feats
in front of the bathroom mirror.
Even as a baby you woke up singing, hands
clapping to a spontaneous song.
One Christmas Eve when our car collapsed
on the frozen highway, you sang your way through
seventeen verses neither of us knew.
Your five-year-old profile, faint against the windshield,
there would be no terror in your song.

This morning, newly married, you sang again
from behind the bedroom door. It was a silly verse
from childhood you wanted me to hear.
But the voice had changed; time itself had changed
what you might become to what you are.
And before dawn, the small, crowded car carried off
the two of you from this coast to the other;
him, tall and cool and silent by his bride.

Skeletons suspended in this sea hold their chests,
rocking their bones up through the foam. The gull
lifts a stranded fish from the crib of rock, and I
take up my book at the edge of this singular horizon.
Yes, I take up my book and begin the formal missing.
But I don't know what is on these pages no matter
how many times I read them, no matter how hard I try.
I only wonder if you're singing now. And why.

JOSEPH STROUD

Below Mount T'ui K'oy,
Home of the Gods,
Todos Santos Cuchumatán,
Guatemalan Highlands

He stumbled all morning through the market,
Drunk and weeping, a young Mayan whose wife
Had died. Whenever he encountered someone he knew,
He'd stop and wail, waving his arms, and try
To embrace them. Most pushed him away,
Or ignored him. So he'd stand there like a child,
Forlorn, his face contorted with grief,
Lost among the piles of corn and peppers,
The baskets of bananas, avocados, and oranges,
The turkeys strung upside down, the careful
Pyramids of chicken eggs, the women
In their straw hats and rainbow *huipils*,
The men smoking cornsilk cigarettes,
Meat hanging from the butchers' stalls
(chorizo, goat heads, tripe, black livers),
As everyone talked, laughed, or bartered,
And young boys played soccer in the courtyard,
The Roman priest, like a thin raven, elbowing
His way through the crowds, rain clouds
Swarming from far down the coast, the sun
Shattered among the pines on the high ranges,
And weaving through all of it the sound
Of women who sang over a corpse in an earthen house,
Keening a music like distant surf breaking
Within the very heart of the mountain.

Signature (V)

Everyone was in the kitchen preparing dinner
When Ellen found her cat under the cabin deck.
It had been dead two weeks. I took a shovel
And crouched between the posts into the damp,
Musky piles of lumber and newspapers.
I tried to pull him out by his hind legs
From beneath a tangle of boards and chickenwire.
He wouldn't budge. Clearing the pile
I discovered he'd plugged his head into the end
Of a pipe. He must have died peering
Through five feet of tunnel toward the dim light
At the end. Like the chimney of hell,
I thought as I pried him loose. The fur
was eaten from around his skull. He looked
Like a Bosch angel—the fluffy,
bloated trunk, white-tipped delicate paws, rigid
Snarled face, teeth bared, milky eyes.
I lifted him out with the shovel and carried him
To the meadow. I had prepared myself for ugliness
And the sick-sweet smell, but was shocked
As the worms dribbled from his mouth.
By now the sun was going down. I buried him
With the light slanting through the madrone and pines.
When I returned to the cabin, a bluegrass tune
Played on the radio, four voice harmony,
Guitar, fiddle, dulcimer, the music
Weaving out through the trees as pollen
Drifted in the fading shafts of light.
I thought of the good earth, and the body's
Slow season. The simple death, and the hard
Death. The burials we are called to.
The roots below in darkness, the flowering
Above in light and air. Love—
Into your company I work my life.

JAN STURTEVANT

Four Progressions

> Memory distills the essence.
> —May Sarton, *I Knew a Phoenix*

1

Stopped for gas in Barstow
we stand outside your car.
"You lied to me," you say. "I'm leaving
you here. Stop crying
or I'm leaving."

Up north, my students wait.
I am four hundred miles
from home.
"Take a bus," you say.
"Walk."

2

Because dinner is cold, and you
are late, your blockish
rage takes us down,
my body strains to get away
mind long gone on disbelief
and these twin terrors:
you could kill me
you could leave me

3

Your anger whips across the room
jerks me up, slaps me
to the wall.
Three days until we marry.

You go outside, swear
at the car, the sun,
the Santa Anas.

Guilt whistles in low tones:
it could be my fault
it could be
it is.

4

In the shelter of the small
of my back, a fist-like
swelling.
I hold myself away from
family, friends. Fear
every embrace, each
hand that lingers, drops
along my waist.

No one must know.
Arm-in-arm, I pose
with you and smile.

AMBER COVERDALE SUMRALL

Black and White . . . Red All Over

My mother's memory is remarkable. She does not allow reality to alter her process of selectively choosing what to preserve, and what to discard or what to edit. She still sends cat food coupons in every letter. My cat died over two years ago.

My mother's cat, Pansy, lived for nineteen years. She was queen of the household. She liked to shit under the flounced sofa or behind the living room drapes. "Pansy had an accident," my mother would say. I would have to clean it up. *Their* relationship was on a much higher level. Pansy spent most of her life on a pillow in my mother's bedroom. When Pansy died, Mother locked her door and sobbed for two days, until my father insisted she come out and cook his supper.

In her "summer" letter, she includes an obituary photo of Doctor Philip McDougal, the Catholic psychiatrist she sent me to when she discovered that I was on the brink of losing my virginity to Danny Guerrero. Dr. McDougal's expressionless face is deeply furrowed. I remember that he never once looked me in the eye. He swiveled endlessly in his brown vinyl chair, puffing on his pipe and occasionally mumbling, "go on, go on." I don't know how he managed to stay awake. Now he's dead of a brain tumor.

My mother hasn't forgotten that I lost my virginity in spite of her intervention. What she has erased from her memory bank is the night Dr. McDougal called her, after my second visit, to say that *she* should be in analysis, not me.

"Sexual desire is normal at sixteen," he told her. "Even for a Catholic girl." I heard him; I was on the other line.

This week her "autumn" letter arrives with the usual assortment of newspaper gleanings and cat food coupons. A photograph of Mrs. Miguel Guerrero floats on top. Now this clipping takes me right back into that sixteen year old Catholic girl.

Danny Guerrero and I are sitting at the card table, holding hands. Our school books are strewn over the living room floor. I have pulled the folding doors closed. The pale blue walls are adorned with religious artifacts: a crucifix, a painting of the Bleeding Heart of Jesus, a statue of the Virgin Mary. More like a shrine than a home.

Every few minutes my mother walks from kitchen to bedroom, then back again. She coughs, clears her throat, asks if we'd like a glass of milk, if we are doing our homework, if it's math or English. Finally, she slides the doors open.

"Your hands should be on the table," she says. "With pencils in them." She tells us she is going to sit and read while we study. "It's too bad you can't be trusted. I have better things to do than be your chaperone."

I'm not permitted to be alone with Danny anymore. We have to double-date or stay home with my parents on the weekends. If we are double-dating, the other couple has to be in Danny's turquoise '56 Buick before he picks me up. Otherwise I stay home.

Danny has already picked Steve and Teresa up. They wave to my mother from Danny's backseat.

"Be home before midnight," she says. "I'll wait up for you."

We drive Steve and Teresa right back to Steve's house and drop them off. We cruise Colorado Boulevard, grab a burger and fries at Bob's then head up Chevy Chase Canyon to our favorite parking spot. We kiss and kiss, hands everywhere, until this is not enough and we unbutton buttons, unsnap snaps, unzip zippers. We are halfway out of our clothes, halfway to paradise, when headlights suddenly appear behind us.

It is my father. Mother has put him on our tail like a bloodhound. She doesn't drive.

"I knew it," she shrieks, when I return, a remnant of myself, in the back of my father's car. "You are leading that boy into pernicious temptation. As surely as Eve led Adam."

"For Christsake, Helen," my father says. "The boy has some responsibility, too."

Mother calls Mrs. Guerrero, arranges a family conference. "We've got real trouble here," she says. "Your son and my daughter are on a collision course straight to Hell."

Danny is on scholastic probation at St. Ignatius. If he wasn't the star quarterback, he'd be expelled already. The conference doesn't include us. We are handed the verdict without an opportunity to present our side. But then, what would it be? Uncontrollable lust? Unbridled passion? Love?

We are forbidden to see or speak to one another. I am threatened with boarding school and grounded for three months.

I have to do all the family ironing as punishment. I iron sheets and pillowcases, handkerchiefs and countless numbers of white shirts. My mother puts Holy Water in the sprinkling bottle. Father Emil gets it for her, like bootleg whiskey.

"To bless the bed," she says. "Keep it pure and white."

"I'm never going to iron sheets when I grow up. Or pillowcases either."

"Then you're inviting the devil into your bed," she says. I deliberately scorch the pure, white sheets. Hold the hot iron down hard until I can smell them burning.

At two in the morning, I am awakened by a soft knocking on my bedroom door. Danny is hiding in the camellias when I open the French-doors.

"I had to see you," he tells me. "I can't stay away." Danny looks like Marlon Brando, only his skin and eyes are darker. He doesn't talk like he has marbles in his mouth though. His eyes narrow to slits when he looks at me sometimes, and a low moan comes from way back in his throat. There is a wildness I cannot resist in him. I write in my diary: We are jungle cats together, driven by unbearable heat.

"I had to see you," he repeats, taking me in his arms.

"No, not here. Wait." I listen for my father's steady snoring then pull the bedspread off the bed and tiptoe out the French-doors. We creep across the backyard, to the patch of lawn hidden behind the juniper bushes where my mother's clothesline stands. Another load of ironing flaps in the cool breeze.

Clothes fly from our bodies as we lie on the damp grass, the bedspread covering us. It is the first time we have been naked together and neither of us can stop trembling. Desire is a fierce ache inside me. Sweet and strong. We roll and toss together until our passion subsides, then sleep as a fine mist begins to fall.

I wake abruptly, to the sound of the kitchen door opening. I hear my mother lift the wire basket of milk, butter, eggs, that the milkman has left. I throw my pajamas on, nudge Danny awake. Last night's romance is light years away. I have to be at school in less than two hours. Danny pulls buttons and zippers frantically.

"Jesus! My dad leaves for work in half an hour." He kisses me then hops over the neighbor's fence. "See you tonight?" he asks.

I nod. "But this time we can't fall asleep. Take a nap or something."

"You'll keep me awake." He winks, then runs back to his Buick parked at the end of the block. As I sneak back to my room, I feel like a vampire who has to be safe in her coffin at first light.

So, this is what "going all the way" is, I'm thinking, as I shower, washing the blood and slick wet from my body. It was a shock to feel Danny so hard, pushing into me. Searing pain, just at first, but then he moaned and shuddered. Stopped moving. It was over so fast, like he went somewhere without me. The best part was the kissing and touching. Maybe tonight will be better.

The worst part is there's no one at school I can tell. News like this would probably reach Mother Superior by lunchtime. My mother would know fifteen minutes later. Thank God I have my diary.

Danny doesn't return that night. Teresa calls, tells me the story. Danny's parents are outside with a police officer when he drives up to his house. The entire neighborhood is outside. They are gathered on Mr. O'Connor's front lawn. Danny does yardwork and odd jobs for Mr. O'Connor. Without him, Danny wouldn't have gas for his car, and we wouldn't be in a constant state of mortal sin.

The swirling beacon of an ambulance bathes Danny in bright red light as he steps out of the car. There is no escape. His father is already moving toward him, fists clenched. Mr. Guerrero hits Danny in the face, knocks him into the street. "You've disgraced our family," he yells. "Mr. O'Connor had a heart attack, was calling for you. You lousy bastard. I know where you were."

He walks away. Danny sits in the street, nose bleeding, lip split open, and wipes the blood and tears on his sleeve. The neighbors are staring and whispering among themselves. His mother, who has been standing at a distance, clutching her rosary beads, hands him a kleenex. "The Lord works in mysterious ways," she tells him softly. "There are no coincidences."

Mercifully, the Guerreros never call my mother. Danny is given a choice: either enter the seminary or transfer to military school. He chooses the latter.

"It's not like we'll never see each other," he tells me, in a pre-arranged phone call. "There's holidays and summer vacation. And in two years we'll get married."

"Oh, sure, Danny. We'll be watched like Russian spies. My mother will hire a private investigator whenever she thinks you're in town. We'll both be dead before we're married."

"I'll find a way," he reassures me. "Nothing will change."

But it already has.

My mother gives me strange, questioning glances. I feel like Hester in *The Scarlet Letter*, indelibly marked as a non-virgin.

"I know what you're up to, young lady," she tells me, arching her long neck and shaking her finger in my face.

"Danny's gone, Mother."

She doesn't believe me, until we run into Mrs. Guerrero one Sunday after Mass.

"Yes, Danny decided to transfer to Army-Navy Academy," she says, never letting on that I'm the reason why. "He needed the discipline."

My mother stops her weird looks. She is confused though. All her senses tell her that I am no longer in a state of grace.

After a flurry of letters, sent via Steve and Teresa, Danny and I meet during Easter vacation. Steve drives all of us to the beach.

Danny's car has been sold by his father to help cover books and tuition. Teresa is pregnant. She and Steve are newly married and living with her parents.

"It's awful," she tells us. "I had to leave school and my friends are acting like I'm contagious or something. Steve and I have no privacy at home. I vomit all morning and sleep all afternoon."

"Yeah, and we have to drive to Griffith Park whenever we want to make love," Steve adds. "Just like before."

I look at Danny, try to imagine living with him, and my mother. "Do you have your nightgown on?" she'd call through the bedroom door. "Have you said your prayers and begged forgiveness from the Blessed Virgin?" I shudder.

Danny's talking to Steve about maybe joining the Marines, seeing some action. He looks at me out of the corner of his eye, as if waiting for me to say, "But Danny, we're planning to get married. Remember?" I say nothing, refuse to meet his eyes. For the first time since I've known him, desire is on the back-burner.

"You remember Mrs. Guerrero," my mother writes. "She died of a massive stroke." I look at the photo again. The clipping accompanying it reads: "Mrs. Miguel Guerrero is survived by her devoted children — Joseph, Daniel, and Maria; and by fourteen grandchildren." My mother has underlined *devoted* and *fourteen*.

I wonder how many of the grandchildren are Danny's. I know he won a football scholarship to Oklahoma State but had to drop out and marry one of the cheerleaders. I wonder if he saw any "action."

"I sent a card conveying our deepest sympathy," my mother continues. "Of course you realize that the seeds for this tragedy were sown years ago." She means me. Danny and me.

I wonder if maybe my mother is thinking that it wouldn't have been so terrible if Danny and I had stayed together. At least she'd have grandkids now. And a Catholic son-in-law. Who knows? I might even be going to Mass on Sundays.

As for me, I'm secretly grateful for her intervention. In Mrs. Guerrero's words, bless her soul, there are no coincidences.

DAVID SWANGER

Bud Vase

It is 1957;
the car is seven years old,
a Chevy in any color we wanted
as long as it was black;
this car was built as a taxi
so we got a deal on everything
but the color. And my license

is new and serious; I carry
it unfolded between sheets
of plastic which are also new
and haven't yet turned yellow.
The Garden State Parkway is
something to be proud of,
pale as a perfect throat
between the corridors of grass.

We close the windows against
our turbulence; your hair cups
its grey, then releases light.
I am driving, you talk across
the long seat, behind the windshield looking toward the road.

I don't want to hear this, but
I am the one driving and you
are the one talking, and you
are telling me about those trips
to New York every week for three
years to be loved by someone.

I thought they were doctor's
visits, a thing intimate
and female needing treatment.
I don't want to hear this,
that in some afternoon apartment
where the air was cleaned
by a low-voiced machine, you managed
a long and careful deception.

But I invent the air conditioner
and the sheets waiting beneath
an expensive blanket; you talk
only of causes, your need for love.
There is no place on the freeway
to stop this from happening;
there is no radio in this car
to turn on. My driving becomes

impeccable; I become the rich lady's
chauffeur, who accelerates the car
to eighty without rippling water
in the bud vase she insists
is a pleasure in her dark limousine.

The Heart's Education

You tell your heart stories;
it cries at the sad parts,
how it is staked in a garden
trying to speak to ripening
versions of itself, a harvest
of red hearts, all hanging
like caught fish: the sun points
its big finger at your heart.

You set your heart afloat
in the cold ribs of the sea:
this too is a lesson in distance,
how the buoys recede like voices,
and the shore becomes unnecessary
while your heart paddles toward
something like itself, turtle-shaped
and wide-eyed and almost obsolete.

You bring your heart into night
where it grips the arm of your chair,
trying to get hold of itself despite
the improbability of happy endings
and the sunset you witnessed,
that huge bruise on the horizon's
forehead, the leaves entering
the forest on their knees.

You show your heart its hydraulic
limits, the weight it can lift
and how it must live by a kind
of harmless burning: you hold
your heart in your hands the way
a fakir holds a coal, ignoring
the complex detonations of flesh,
your heart's bright teeth.

ROBERT SWARD

Taking a Photo

I lie there watching her
Through it, bored, timid lover
With Kodak, wanting to make
A stranger of her. I scratch
and keep on watching her.
It is like a photograph. It *is*,
But it does not occur to me
To take—or to throw away
The Kodak. I hold it there
Between us and try to see her.
She's turned the other way.
She smiles without looking at me.
I close my eyes on her
And love her, click the shutter.
I take her photograph.
I take six. "It is like love,"
I say. "It doesn't move me,
Not one bit," she says.
"You're invisible," she says.

MARK TAYLOR

Glaciers

The day begins in sunlight.
My father comes to smoke
and compliments my tan.
The birds are perched in walnut trees.
And a lifetime of resentment chills the day.
My father says he hasn't forgotten
the time I yelled at him for no reason
two years ago. I close my eyes.
He says he stays away from me now.
And I start to cry.
Upset, he reaches out to touch my arm,
but I am not crying because of what he said
today. I am crying because he and I are
glaciers of emotion, deep, and unthawed.
We are descended from ice ages past,
and we have not emerged from long periods
of frozen time. He offers me a valium
and says someone told him it's good to cry.
And I start to laugh through my tears
knowing this is just one breath
between long eons of glaciation.

LOUISE THORNTON

Summer of My Seventh Year

We come home through the stars,
through the thicket of moths and fireflies
swarming in the dark
when no one is there but
Annie and I riding,
gravel thudding against the bottom of the car
miles into the cradled dark.
The moon follows beside us
filtering the fields across fences,
across cows grazing in white splendor
in the still spaces,
bathing my hand on the window's edge,
Aunt Annie beside me,
frogs singing in the damp grasses
milk night all around.

PATRICE VECCHIONE

Pam's Getting Married, and I'm a Little Pink

Your father will be the preacher,
mustached and heavyset.
You'll wear off-white, stand
straight and smile.
In a back row I'll get teary.
Seventeen years ago we married only
each other and our fantasy
grooms, the grown-up boy
whose thigh I stroked. I could feel
the blood surge beneath
his pants, under his skin.
We wanted their lips, their thick
wet lips. Knowing desire, we slept with
it between us, whispering
our futures.

All the years between then and now evaporate.
It's been one long dream
and I'm getting older.
The promise of wrinkles
forms around my lips, above
my eyebrows. I apply the many creams.
Your hair is unnaturally curly,
and truly blond.

This isn't dress-up anymore.
My mother is buried, and her shoes
are still too large.
This is the real thing. At the party
we won't get up and dance
together like the young,
single girls we were
in our wide skirts, jutting hips
and our sudden breasts
for the sky and everyone to see.

The Sadness I Live For

Grandmother's teeth sleep
without her in the blue box
beside the bathroom sink.
They greet me
at night in their shiny silence
when I stumble
across the aging floorboards
of my grandmother's house.

Grandma, those porcelain teeth
will outlive you
and I cannot listen to them speak
of traveling across Manhattan by horse.
I cannot fit them in my own
mouth when you are gone, gone.

Early summer mornings you
wheel out to the livingroom
for your daily shave,
your ancient legs half covered.
No teeth this early and you
become my Mr. Magoo, Casper the
Ghost, my only hero.
The electric razor buzzes your
chin clean.

Then it's breakfast and another
television day beside
the rumbling air conditioner.
I fall asleep in your presence
and dream of you only twenty-five
years ago, the fine grandma
you were, your spaghetti noodles
drying on the bed.

This year you will give me
maybe one more story, and I will
ask for it over and over, again.
I will tell you stories of
the family I met last summer in
the old country, the woman
who has grandpa's very own
face, my skin, my skin, yours.

You will hand me another
string of pearls left over from
the thin years of tripe for dinner
and a bean soup, when you strung
beads for money.
The fake strand will be longer this
year as I am older, more deserving of
your gems and the gold-threaded
dresses I am too thin to wear.

Grandma, you are our history
alive. And when you are gone you
will be more than my hero, you
will be the end of a world.
You will be the sadness
I live for.

ALMA LUZ VILLANUEVA

Matrix

On the curve of the freeway
onramp a small, dark
figure is illuminated by my
headlights—the face,

a patch of anxiety—
blonde, young, pretty—
pick me up, pick me up—
please—

I think of the man who'll
pick her up if I don't
and I shudder—she
could be my granddaughter

ten years from now—
she could be dead
ten minutes from now—
I stop.

Thanks for the ride,
she says—Women
don't usually pick
up other women, she

smiles at me, shyly.
That's pretty dangerous,
I say, standing there,
in the dark, by yourself.

My car broke down
after ten years, $700
to fix it, may as
well get another one,
it was a VW bus, good
car, yeah, found out
today I have diabetes,
guess it's better than
cancer, right? I guess
it's better than cancer,
still I have to get
used to it, I'm going
to my girlfriend's house,
feel like talking to some
one, have to hitchhike, sure
is funny to be without
a car after ten years,
I had a hysterectomy
after four years of pain,
so I could hardly stand
and I was working at a
fast food place walking
on cement all day, kept
going from doctor to doctor
until they finally took
it out, the pain. . . .

The small, soft pain
of womanhood standing
in the night, in the dark,
waiting for a ride,

my womb aches for
you, the kotex I just
replaced catches its
quota of fresh birth

blood—I, the older
woman still bleed, still
have my compass to guide
me, and I worry for
you, young woman, how
you'll find your way
without your dark, sweet
matrix, ebbing and cresting,

within you—the small,
soft pain of womanhood
I picked up and placed,
so carefully, in my

womb—I saw you standing
there, alone, in the matrix
of the darkest night—we
will find our way.

T. MIKE WALKER

Lebanon: L'École Technologic Orphanage, 1978

excerpt from *The Last American*

Ara trudged over rubble in the streets of West Beirut in 1978, staring at the children playing in the ashes, their hands reaching out, their mothers mouthing curses as they huddled in doorways of their bombed out multi-level apartment houses. The sky was filled with flares and sirens which cut in and out of the women's wailing.

Swimming south through Sidon in a red sea of pain, Ara took the bloody coast road to Mostafa's orphanage, L'École Technologic, in Tyre, Lebanon, where tanks rumbled over crater-torn roads and teenage boys in camo-clothes carried rifles and machine guns.

In Mostafa's apartment, he looked out at the huge Israeli gunboats in the bay as they bombed the Palestinian camp which was hidden in the vast orange groves and ripe Lebanese orchards which stretched from ten kilometers south of Tyre all the way north to Sidon in one of the richest, most productive lands on earth. Flashes of flame in the camp were followed by muffled explosions which shook the orphanage on its hillside three kilometers away. Already the bodies of burned and wounded Palestinians and Lebanese were being driven or carried to the orphanage, where the basement had become an infirmary and the halls were lined with groaning bodies and grieving people.

Mostafa rushed to the building and opened a switchbox on the wall, flicking out all lights except for the emergency system in the basement and lower halls. "They use our school to line up their tracers on the camp, because we are the tallest building in town. Of course, we cannot permit that. They must furnish their own light to commit their hellish deeds. Look—the snake strikes."

He pointed toward the bay where a sleek black Cobra helicopter swooped in from the boats, heading directly for the school. "They hate us, but they dare not destroy us completely. Even Israel is sensitive to world opinion, and for them to blow up an orphanage would be unforgivable. They have attacked several times with tanks and mortars, but more to punish us than to eliminate us completely—although that is what they would like most to do."

The chopping sound of the blades grew louder until it roared around their ears. To Ara's amazement, the US Navy- built Bell helicopter flew directly up to the window where Ara stood watching. Ara dove for the floor, but Mostafa shook his fist at the pilot.

"Nazis!" He shouted through the glass to the pilot's deaf ears.

Instead of machine-gunning them, the helicopter rose straight up and fired a flare which arched high up over the school and burst like a supernova into red light, bathing the buildings and surrounding hills with the color of blood.

"Now I know why your wife and children moved back to California," Ara shouted from the floor. "How can you stand this crap, Mostafa? What are you even doing here? I thought you were a man of peace, a mystic! What does this battle have to do with your own country, your own struggle. Lebanon is just crazy as far as I can see."

"Perhaps you don't see far enough," Mostafa said, sadly, and helped Ara off the floor. "You see only the outer. But if you seek peace, work first for justice." Mostafa scratched his neatly trimmed black beard. "Imam Mussa called me here to undertake a great task which requires my complete attention and dedication. Either one is born into these conditions or one willingly undertakes them to serve a greater purpose. I have lived with these bombings since 1974, but it was my wife's choice to return to America. I could not blame her, nor did I try to stop her. It is true that I have four children by her and my heart breaks to think of them, but I also have four hundred children here with no one to take care of them. I assure you that this is my fight too, and if you could only see the situation through my eyes you would know it is your fight as well. In Lebanon, life and death are like mirrors locked face to face."

"But how can anyone stand it? All day long, all night."

"They can't. They go crazy with rage, or they become apathetic. Half the Shia youth from the south have moved to Beirut. They said 'to hell with this life,' and who can blame them? But not everyone has the choice to move."

"It seems absolutely hopeless."

"Each person must answer that question for himself. I will tell you a story. God was lonely. The whole of the Universe — the Angels, the Stars, all worshipped Him, but no one recognized His Greatness, His Essence. So he created man in his image to recognize Him — gave man beauty, power, creation, love, everything in order to recognize Him. Gave him pain to bake his heart, gave him sorrow to simmer his soul, gave him loneliness to be perfect in all the attributes of God. Without loneliness, man would not be perfect. Love prepares you for the loneliness. Worldly love must be broken in order to find the path. Man is destined to be lonely. Therefore it is in this loneliness that man meets God, which forms the basis for Unity and Oneness. Therefore, loneliness and pain are the bliss of God, and the path of separation yields the Higher Unity."

Outside fires raged, explosions slammed against the hills, the air was filled with sirens.

SARA WALSH

Boulder Creek   1985

Water hisses.
I pour tea,
hum to hear myself,
louder
to match the wail of wind,
thunder.

I have heard it before,
known trees to scratch window
panes to tremble,
earth to slide.
Gusts of ashes
cough at the hearth,
fingers tap glass.

Rain returns.

Deadwood branches
choke the creek,
lift the stream
to gnaw at my doorstep.

The guest no longer welcome
knocks again:
I rise to answer
the stream and hillside
rush to embrace.
I rise as steam.

KEN WEISNER

Just Like We Did

"And the rainbow had a storm just like we did."
— jww 4/14/86

And the storm had an elevator
       elevator had a cow in it just like we did
       cow had people in it
       people had brains in them just like we did
       brains ideas
       ideas sounds,
       sounds taps, and the taps
syncopations just like we were,
       storms crescendos and arpeggios just like we did
       rainbow had a storm
       leaves had telephones and countries just like we had
       faces were water
       sounds had fish in them just like we did
       fish had colors and the çolors lights
       lights had dust in them just like we were
       dust had planets and the planets moons
       moons songs
and the songs had children
       songs had children in them just like we were.

STEVE WIESINGER

Simple Answers

Duncan zipped the child in his sweater jacket. Taking walks together was new, and usually Duncan was too absorbed for much play. But today there was a fallen pine tree in their path.

The boy climbed along the trunk in his miniature yellow work boots. Then he turned, and making absolutely certain his father stood in place, jumped to his outstretched hands.

Duncan set the boy at his feet. "You want to go again?" The boy scampered back to where the roots broke from the earth in contorted shapes. Duncan moved alongside as the boy used branches to balance on the mottled bark. "Catch me, daddy."

Duncan eased a pace backward. "Jump to me."

"No," the child protested. "You come here, like before."

Duncan compromised half a step.

"It's too far," the child wailed.

"You think I'm going to let you hit the ground?"

Finally, the child launched himself, his dark curly hair filling with wind. Duncan caught his compact weight, swung him sideways toward a duck pond, then flipped him upside down and over, setting him back on the fallen tree. The child was amazed to find himself on his feet, back where he started.

"Again. Do it again." The child bounced with excitement, and for one moment, the heaviness Duncan carried from work to automobile to apartment to single bed lifted.

The next week walking together, Duncan set him on a rock near the shoreline. The boy was strongly affected by the separation, and the teachers at his pre-school repeated stories of the boy's withdrawal. Duncan didn't want to screw him up any worse, but the ache was too much to overcome. "You know your mom and I are living separate," he said. "What do you think it was that I did wrong?"

The child ceased his movements, seemed to retreat into his

pale skin and dark curly hair. "I don't know."

"Maybe something you saw — with your eyes?"

The boy took a child's breath, "Whenever you had a fight, you were always the winner."

The apartment was a converted motel room — one room facing the driveway-courtyard, a tiny bathroom with a rusting metal shower stall, a slender hallway that connected to a rear kitchen with a shrunken refrigerator and stove. Duncan was learning to cook. He made kid's food for the boy — peas, chicken, turkey legs, hamburgers. One of the disputes between he and Amelia had been Kevin's refusal to eat, rebelling at her beef stroganoff and tofu broccoli. For six months all Kevin would put in his mouth were toasted cheese sandwiches. The constipation had been epic.

Amelia hadn't much liked the bathing battle, either. So now after dinner, Duncan stood the howling child under the shower and attempted to apply soap to his slippery skin, to shampoo his hair. The fourth go around, right when Duncan was preparing to give it up, the boy submitted. "My dad's teached me to take a shower," Kevin announced one bathing session when a neighbor stopped in.

Each night after the boy was encased in his sleepers, his pale cheeks shiny, his hair brushed out with No More Tangles, Duncan lacked the energy to do his stained glass or anything else. But the chores gave him the opportunity to picture Amelia's pleased expression, drink up her imaginary praise. "God, he looks so cute. How do you get him to hold still?"

Amelia was also surprised he had consented to taking the child half-time. One of her favorite pre-separation jabs revolved around a picture the kid had painted at day care. Asked to explain the lines and squiggles, the boy had said: "That's my daddy working. He works all day and night, too. Someday he's going to play with me."

Now Amelia would tell Duncan how wonderful his new attitude was. "I never thought you had it in you. My friends can't believe it."

"I guess I never tried enough before." Duncan chose his words carefully. "My father never paid any attention to us — you've seen him—he's not much for kids. So I just improvise now with Kevin."

Yet instead of winning her back, his efforts boomeranged. The child had been her prime concern for four years, six months—nine extra months counting the pregnancy. But now that Duncan accepted more responsibility, she took to heavy-duty socializing. Even after she broke up with her boyfriend, she ditched the child with sitters every night. She freely admitted she was regressing to her early twenties which she had missed because of marriage.

It drove Duncan crazy. All his life he had felt an odd, aching hole in his middle. Mostly, he could ignore it. But this deal opened it up crater-sized, and his entire being felt like it was sliding in at the edges.

At night, after the child was asleep, he took a two-liter bottle of Burgundy and anesthetized himself, ranting at her one minute, too sad to sleep the next, knowing that by any measure his mistakes in the marriage were worse than whatever she was doing now.

"God is dead," the boy said. They stepped outside to the driveway-courtyard, were on their way to the store.

"What did you say?" Duncan asked.

The boy mumbled something into the miniature scarf Duncan had looped around his neck.

"What?" Duncan asked.

"He's buried under the ground."

Duncan bent his six foot frame toward the kid. "I don't understand. Who's under the ground?"

"God." The boy's round cheeks and green eyes were void of expression, as though everyone knew this fact. "He's thirty feet under the ground."

Duncan peered at the mixture of beach clapboard, fancy designer, and 40's ranch style homes along 26th Avenue. For a moment, he was haunted with a strange vacancy, as though the spirit had leaked out of the sky and earth.

"But why is he under the ground?" Duncan asked as they continued toward the mom and pop grocery.

"Because everything is made. The trees, the telephone poles, the houses. It's all done, he doesn't have anything more to do, so they buried him." The boy spoke the last words with effort. Then he squirmed his pudgy fingers into Duncan's hand. "Can I get candy?"

It was nightfall. Months had sagged together. Duncan was feeling unusually poor as he steered the old '75 Dodge Dart across town via the beach route. He'd picked up the child from pre-school, fed him, entertained him, and now was delivering him, special favor, to Amelia. She'd been involved with meetings all afternoon. At this moment in Duncan's mind, she'd just returned home and was getting out of the shower, skin warm from the hot water. It seemed that everytime he picked up or delivered the kid, she was in some wrenching state of undress.

"What are the stars made of?" the boy asked from his second hand car seat in the rear. He had been chirping all afternoon. His questions reached Duncan like a snatch of lyrics from a song on the radio.

"Well," he replied, "they're like our sun." Half-way through his explanation he bogged down. Last night, she had spoken the word divorce. At work today, his hand had shaken so badly that he'd screwed up the figures in every last assessment.

"But where do the stars come from?" the boy insisted. "Who made the stars?"

"I don't know." He roused himself to answer. "Some people say it was God. They think God made all the stars and the earth and everything." Coming to a red light, he turned and glanced at the child in the car seat which was cracking and losing its foam. "Other people say it just happened. You know, there were gases and explosions and everything just came together, almost by mistake." He let out the clutch and followed traffic across the bridge, his thoughts sliding toward the dim night that awaited him in the apartment. These were the kind of nights where he nearly had to tie himself down from driving past their Victorian, checking her lighted bedroom window.

"But where did God come from?"

"Kevin, these are really good questions." He adjusted the rear view mirror so he could see the child. "People have asked questions like that all through history—smart people, grown up people. And there aren't necessarily answers, you understand? Your answers are just as good as anyone's, even the smartest people of all time."·

The child nodded, a pleased, goofy expression on his face.

"See," Duncan continued, "Some people say that people make up God, because they want answers to these questions, and God seems like an answer. But other people say, whoa, no dice, where did everything come from if there wasn't a God? Something had to start it all. So these people say that God always existed, and He's the force that created everything else."

The boy seemed to consider this, though it was difficult to tell with his goofy expression. "Whose side are you on, daddy?"

Duncan braked at the last stop light. "I don't know." His breath came out of him as though someone had jumped on his stomach. "Sometimes I think one way and sometimes another."

"I don't know either," the boy declared happily.

The child's tone revived him; why not be undecided? "Here's one for you, though," Duncan said, "If God is dead—you know, buried under the ground," he glided up in front of the Victorian which day by day was becoming more foreign, "so if He's buried, and God is the force that makes everything, how can everything go on?"

The boy still wore his smile.

"You want to get out?" Duncan asked.

"Yes!" The child began kicking to get free of the seat. "Mommy, mommy," he called as Duncan extricated him from the straps.

Kevin scampered toward the front door. In the oval portal over the door stood one of Duncan's pieces: a pair of seagulls wheeling through azure sky. Duncan hesitated, took a step inside. The air smelled of spaghetti sauce and carried a male voice.

Waves lapped on the sand, strewing dirty puffs of foam. They looked like used-up soad suds. The child liked to stomp on them with his yellow workboots.

"I'm tired, daddy."

Duncan swung the boy to his shoulders. With Kevin's hands

in his hair, he started toward the apartment. In an hour, they would leave on the drive for his parents' home. It had been six months since he and Amelia separated, and it was time to let his parents know about the decisions. The only positive thing to tell them was that he actually enjoyed the half time taking Kevin. Anyway, he would have dinner, spend the night, and let his mother provide some comfort. Meanwhile, the boy chattered about stars and tides. A retired neighbor smiled at them, father and son on the windy beach. Yeah, that's all, Duncan muttered.

As he trudged across the sand, a memory surfaced—how his parents once came on a vacation to this same beach, his father's Korean War flight jacket and stolid shape. The leathery, impenetrable feel of his calloused palm.

Then right at the access road the park service used, with Kevin's firm, sausage ankles in his hands, Duncan was swept with a moment of absolute clarity. No Amelia. No despair. Usually he thought in pictures, but this was his voice, reverberating in the chambers of his ears as though it had been pre-recorded. The words unrolled with such precision he stopped cold: "This is my son. He needs me as much as I needed my father."

"Come on, daddy," Kevin banged with his heels. "Let's go see grandma."

ANITA WILKINS

Beyond Piute Pass

It's cold here.
This stone basin. Peaks
ground to a glacial edge.
We climbed a long time to get here,
past lodgepoles and aspens,
Mt. Emerson's rust-red cliffs,
its blunt-faced matterhorn.
Past the precipitous walls of
the Inconsolable Range.
Over Piute Pass into these cirques,
lakes like cold eyes,
this simplification. Water
and ice, the skyline of rock.
The small toad, composite gray and black
like a piece of granite broken off
and hopping away. The few stunted plants
growing alone where distance
is absolutely required. Here
whatever puts down roots and sends up leaves
hurries, because even now there's snow on the wind.

Here words like "endurance"
take on the hard rhythms of our walking,
of the lungs' struggle for breath at this height.
Other words like "tenderness" or "grief"
pitch like rubble at the foot
of these mountains or
come back moaning to our cold ledge
when I wake up under the stars.

By day the sky is fragile
over the sharp-minded peaks.
We hurry in a great lethargy.
What am I afraid of here?
That we crawl
like spiders in this bowl of rock,
light filling the bowl morning after morning?
That Piutes who passed here
left less trace than
the wind leaves, working at rock?

No, that the mountain grows up
inside us. That morning
comes to this high place
and includes us. That step by step
the habit of rock hardens.
We take on the colors of granite.
We can stare upward
a long time now without blinking,
our eyes like cold lakes
under the inconsolable sky.

The Time Goes On Being Broken

Last night from Eftalou in the back
of the blue Mazda truck, we rode
with the empty fish crates.
The moon shone down on us
and a cool wind blew.
Your guitar strings spoke to us
a few times in its case
as the truck bumped
over the graveled road.
We hardly said anything.
Phillada talked a little
in Greek, something in English,
inconsequential.
Behind us in Eftalou
the taverna was closing.
It was three a.m. or later.
Off to our right, the sea
and the mountains of Turkey
rode with us all the way back.

The August moon is no longer full.
One side gets smaller
each night like my time here.
I leave at the middle of the month
near an old anniversary, a young man's
deathday. He was my husband, my love,
too many years ago now
to remember exactly what August day it was.
You'll fade, too, like that
into a darkness where the heart
goes dead and must be brought back to life again
somehow, when that seems not possible.

We came home last night. We slept.
This morning again, too early,
you got up, went to work.
You'll come home at four o'clock, tired.
We'll swim. You'll sleep.
Nothing happens out of the ordinary.
Except your hands. Your mouth.
You look at me. I touch you.

The moon gets smaller.
Every day the road to Eftalou
gets hotter and more bleached,
the thistles in the fields grow sharper,
and the time goes on being broken.

KIRBY WILKINS

Rain Shadow

He hadn't seen another human for six days, and it wasn't easy. The Sierra had become so popular, he sometimes wondered why bother. But by staying off the trails, skirting lakes where there might be fishermen, scrambling up ridges to camp high, he'd managed solitude. Distant voices once and a campfire, but nothing else. The week alone had cleared his mind, and he saw his life for what it was—overcrowded with material possessions and social events. He and Ruth pretended otherwise, but their marriage was a husk. He looked forward to a real purge upon his return.

It was a bright evening as Jack stepped onto a main trail, his beard greyer than he realized without a mirror this past week. He moved easily in his solitude. Tied outside his orange pack was a sleeping mat made from the same material that kept re-entering satellites from burning up in the atmosphere. Inside the pack were thermal underwear, down parka, stove that produced 10,000 BTU on 6 oz. of fuel, several foil packets of freeze-dried food, powdered high-energy drinks concocted for astronauts, a nesting set of aluminum pans, teflon fry pan, snakebite kit, Swiss army knife with corkscrew and miniature scissors, and 100 feet of high test climbing rope. In the map pocket was a set of topographical maps and a slim volume of Zen Buddhist koans. He was feeling very fit and clear when he made his first contact with humans.

Four people stood in a cluster at a bend of the trail. As Jack approached, one of them, a boy, held out his hand and made quick patting gestures toward the trail. It was almost hallucinatory, as if the boy had been expecting him, and Jack stopped abruptly before he understood the signal—that he was to approach slowly and cautiously.

When he was close enough, the boy whispered, "Do you know what it is?"

Jack stared at a grey bird clutching a grey boulder within arm's reach of any of them. It was a nondescript bird that he was sure he had seen, but had never thought to name since he had little interest in bird life.

"We think he's injured," one of the older boys said. They were vigorous, athletic-looking boys, high school and college athletes he would guess, and their concern for a mere bird surprised Jack. He looked more closely. The drab bird was swiveling its head, pecking into cracks, and seemed healthy enough, but its behavior *was* odd, as though it wanted to be near people yet was feigning indifference to them.

"It's not identified in our book," the oldest boy said. He was holding a *Field Guide to Western Birds*.

"It looks pretty common to me," Jack said.

"Well, it's not." The older man spoke sharply without turning his head, and for the first time Jack looked at him closely. In profile, the face was haggard and unshaven, not uncommon in hikers, but also rigid like a mask. "It's eating seeds out of the cracks. Look under seedeaters," he commanded the young man with the book.

"They aren't classified that way, Father."

Father. So the trailside tableau had a name: Father and Sons Studying an Unidentified Bird.

"Look under drab," Jack said.

The boys were inclined to be amused, but looked first at their father as though spontaneous humor might be profane. Jack followed their eyes for a second close look at the man, his face still obstinately fixated on the bird. This time the pallor of the man's skin struck Jack. It was precisely as grey as the rock or the bird. It was not the face of a man inclined to be amused.

Since the bird continued to do nothing more remarkable than swivel its head and peck into cracks, Jack hitched up his pack and began to edge past the group. It was clear the old man did not welcome an intruder witnessing their communion. But when Jack moved, the man looked sharply at him, and the bird sprang from the rock. It flicked its wings and pulled away in a tight upward spiral like a grey wisp of smoke emerging from the man's skull. The sons and Jack followed its flight, while the man stared at Jack.

"It's okay, Father," one of the boys said. "He's flown away."

The father turned. Jack began walking once again. When he glanced back, the four figures were also descending, the boys clustered around the man who seemed hunched over himself. A sick man, Jack realized. Very sick. Since they carried no packs, the family must have camped nearby and taken an evening stroll. He had not thought to ask. Behind the descending family the sky was unsettled—a high, fast haze spreading from the southwest. He did not look back again.

That night he camped in the open where he could watch the sky. After eating, he sat beside his fire and watched the swift overcast reach out over the eastern deserts. He slipped into his bag and tried to imagine whether Ruth were asleep or watching TV in the lamplight, or even whether she had come home.

When he awoke, no stars were visible overhead, but the atmosphere around him was faintly luminescent, as if the granite were radioactive. Wind roared over the pass and wuthered high up the ridge, but the lower forest was still. The radioactive light was caused by a third-quarter moon rising above the cloud cover. It was a moon which had shone on his face all week.

He lay waiting for the changes that preceded rain, glad the weather had held off till this last day. A few more hours would be convenient, but on the lee side of the Sierra and only a few hours walk from his car, it was not important. He imagined the mountains he had just crossed rising up and obstructing the free movement of air across thousands of miles of open Pacific. All winter, storms would crash on the west side of the range like great breakers, one after another. Ths was the first fall storm, but he lay secure on the dry side of the range. In the rain shadow.

At grey dawn, the first drops sprinkled over him, and breaking camp quickly, he ate one of the high-energy snacks designed for astronauts. Feeling fit and clear-headed, with the storm pursuing him and the first grey light turning the granite grey like storm waves, he walked swiftly down through the wet trees that were becoming grey-green in the early light. The dust of the trail was packed black and impressionable under foot, and the following wind blew smells of an early fall down from the high country.

Because of the wind he didn't hear the man behind him until he felt a hand on his shoulder. A tremendous surge of adrenalin pumped through him as he whirled, stumbling and ready to fight, not wanting this to happen, not here in the solitude of the mountains. But it was only the middle son, breathing hard and leaning over like an exhausted runner. "Do you have any oxygen?" he asked.

Still trembling and white-lipped, Jack felt his face rigid with fear . . . and the effort not to show it.

"Oxygen?"

"He's having trouble breathing and . . . we thought . . . because you were older . . . perhaps . . . "

Rain spiraled crazily down over both of them. "Oxygen?" he repeated, shaking his head.

The boy stood up straight, and Jack remembered his father's hostile face, his grey lifeless eyes. "Can I help?" he asked.

"Our other brother went ahead for help. There are still two of us."

The other brother must have passed while Jack was still asleep. Heart attacks, he knew, often came in the morning. "Are you sure?"

The boy shook his head. It was the moment to insist, of course, but the son was shaking his head wildly, refusing. "If you see my brother, tell him to hurry."

Then he began to run back up the trail. Jack watched him disappear before he turned back down the trial, his own heart beating frantically and unevenly. As he descended into swirling mist, he heard the invisible trees roaring all around him like fire and saw greasy-wet boulders rising up like undersea animals.

This time he heard boots grating on gravel and turned before the boy could touch him. The careless way the boy's feet were stumbling and slipping made Jack's chest constrict with a new fear. The boy's eyes were unfocused and wild, but devoid of tears. His face was slick with rain. This time he did not stop.

"He died," he said, passing Jack. And then from further down the trail added: "After you left." Or that's what it sounded like.

He ran on around a bend in the trail, leaving Jack alone once again. So a single son remained with his dead father. A lonely vigil.

Jack should walk back into the storm to sit with the boy. But the trail was steep and wet, the storm roared. How could he help? These people were strangers. Only strangers. There was nothing he could do. So he continued down between stone walls and soon emerged in a softer region where the pretty little aspen leaves raged like waterfalls. The leaves were autumn-bright and their presence was soothing. He slowed his pace, thinking of the austere mountains he had always loved, so clear and so simple, and the dead man lying up there.

A slight figure came running up the trail—the youngest son who had asked him to identify the bird and had gone ahead for help. His older brother must have caught up and sent him back.

"I'm sorry," Jack said when the boy was close enough to hear over the wind.

He was sobbing, snot running down his face, clothes soaking wet. He stared at Jack without recognition.

"He was okay . . . all week . . . then his breathing . . . got funny."

"It's the altitude," Jack said. "It's hard on the heart."

The boy looked at him. "My father is dead."

Before Jack could offer any conventional condolences, the boy began to run uphill. Once again, Jack was left alone to continue his descent from the high country. His boots pressed into the trail, making distinct prints. Sagebrush appeared looking like beaten pewter. The clouds had begun to lift.

The helicopter passed low overhead as if on a strafing run, the thunk, thunk of the blades interrupting his thoughts. He'd been imagining the body brought out on a horse, the sons walking in the rain with their breath and the animal's mingling in the chill air. But of course that was foolish in the modern era.

It did not seem possible for the pilot to land in such weather and such forbidding terrain, but soon enough the helicopter returned like a spider in the sky, and he remembered the many pilots trained in Vietnam who were flying commercially now. Evacuating a single body without concern for enemy fire must be ludicrously simple. He wondered whether the boys rode inside, or whether they had to come out on foot. He wondered if they saw him down below, or even cared to look. He wondered how they would transport the corpse across California.

In his car, windshield wipers working steadily, he turned on the radio and heard the news. It was only a reflex because after a week's solitude in the mountains, he really didn't care what had happened in the world. In his absence, millions of new images had been imprinted on the human mind. Viking had landed on Mars. Conditions suitable for life had not yet been found, but the photographs were stunning and of great scientific importance. He would see them on television that evening, the surface of Mars. He turned off the radio and sat back.

Although cold rain swirled in broken curtains across the desert, the car was warm. It was two hundred miles back to the coast and a much milder fall. But already the solitude of the mountains had been replaced by something else—this solitude inside his car. He wondered what would come for him? Just the helicopter descending like a claw? Or the grey wisp of an anonymous bird? Through the windshield greasy with road slime, he was staring at a slick, black road.

CARTER WILSON

Captain Soto and His Friends

In the old days, Leo Soto was universally considered the best pilot in town. The story was that when U.S. airlines began running short of experienced crews during World War II, they took young men up from south of the border to train, and the process had given Mexico its one generation of truly great airmen, including, of course, San Martín's own Captain Soto.

Still, people always advised travelers to be sure to get away by noon. After that, especially in summer, steely clouds rushed in over the mountains around town. What people avoided saying was that after midday every minute that passed diminished the likelihood of *any* of the local pilots remaining sober.

Only Captain Soto offered any guarantee on his work. If he could get out to his little Cessna under his own steam, he promised, he would land you anywhere in the state of Chiapas.

As befit a small-town celebrity, he was pointed out in bars. An unusually tall man in his middle forties with a pencil mustache, a John Barrymore nose and damp but impenitent eyes, the Captain occupied the place of honor at his friends' table. Back to the wall amidst their raucous flapping, Soto remained taciturn, sometimes even bleak looking in his solitude.

His friends were all men he had grown up with. As boys in the Thirties they had dreamed together they would some day become good enough at something—anything would do—to escape the stagnation of the provinces. Chiapas was a subject of cosmopolitan jest. If you insisted you *had* to have a ticket for Tuxtla, the state capital, fifty-some air miles and 6,000 feet down the escarpment from San Martín, the clerk would look blandly at you and say, "Why? Nothing going on there anyway."

At some point late in the evening, Umberto, the one who covered *futbol* for the local paper, would inevitably propose a toast 'To the idiocy of rural life!' And when all had drunk, just as inevitably

Umberto would add, 'As Carlitos Marx so *rightly* called it.' They were aging bohemians far from Bohemia, and if they often acted more like barbarians, it did not take much to understand their neglect of their families and their sometimes cruel pranks as a form of fitful protest. Cheated or incapable of what they imagined would be meaningful lives, Captain Soto's friends had undertaken a guerrilla action against meaning itself.

The principal weapon in their arsenal was talk. Off and on for fourteen hours one day I listened to them discuss whether or not there was such a thing as the idea of a horse chestnut in the Spanish spoken in Spain, given their general agreement that the horse chestnut tree does not grow in Spain. At the six hour mark the one they called the Artist, who carried charcoal pencils in the breast pocket of his shiny gabardine suit and one time or another had taught at every convent school in the state, was still maintaining that, although he conceded the non-existence of the thing in Spain, the *concept* must still exist because he had once seen the word "horse chestnut" in the unimpeachable dictionary of the Spanish Academy. The eventual resolution of the issue came from whoever it was who framed the immortal sentence, '*Existe, pero no hay,*' which may be glossed as 'It [the notion of horse-chestnutness] exists, but there aren't any [that is, actual horse chestnuts in Spain].'

I sometimes wondered why Soto, the only one of them who possessed the means of escape, had never fled to fame and glory, or at least to some bigger town. Maybe it was out of loyalty to his old pals. Or it may be he stayed because Chiapas' windy limestone mountains and its rain forests with their stingy landing facilities were the right places to continue practicing his special art.

The Captain favored economy. Going to the lowlands, he rose only high enough to clear the rim of San Martín's bowl, then descended in one long skimming tack. The Cessna would pass just barely above one ridge and the rows of corn would be dropping away under you, the Indians and the chickens and sheep getting smaller, and there would be the silver wiggle of a river in the bottomland and then all at once the far side would come rushing at you, the dropping-away film playing in reverse too fast so it looked as though Soto had misjudged, and just when you were about to shout at him *Pull up, man, pull up!* he'd squeak over the top and the next valley would already be dropping away, while back along the last ridge the pinetops would still be waving frantically in your wake. All this to save gas.

He also appeared to enjoy heightening small dramas. Once, coming in past the weddingcake ruins at Palenque, we encountered a large brahmin bull occupying the dusty airstrip. So the Captain buzzed the field. Once, twice — we passengers hanging on like the smaller aerialists in the trapeze act's grand finale — when, at the top of his third swing, he pulled the throttle all the way out, which stalled the engine. We went into a dead silent glide down toward the ground. The Captain throttled back in. *Nada.* The strip was coming up. The bull was loping away. Soto felt up onto the dashboard like an orderly in Emergency groping inside a shirt for a bad ticker, made a fist and hit the metal one mighty blow. The engine kicked back in and we made ready to land.

The Captain was married to a small, pretty woman who had presented him with nearly a dozen plump babies over the years. Her neighbors judged her lot a particularly sorry one. Bad enough never knowing *when* your husband might come home to supper, poor Sra. Soto had to contend also with *if.* She was given to counting her youngest children over and over with her eye, as though someone was already missing, and to preparing *Royal Flan de Caramel Instante* in the afternoon and then eating it all herself. So mournful a lady, in fact, that even for some years before Leo's untimely death she was known about town as 'The Widow Soto'.

As no one could resist saying, her weeds became her. She grew again as lively as she had been as a girl. She began renting out rooms to foreigners and other interesting people and she was always so *glad* when you dropped by, and would take you in at once to view Leo's photograph on the mantel above the electric log. The Captain of this portrait was poignantly fresh, a young man yet, you might say, to test his wings on the updrafts of life.

Yes, the Señora would say, awful about her poor dear Leo. But God's will *is* God's will, and *she* agreed with those who said he was not a bad man, only a man cursed with bad friends.

Not everyone put the whole blame for what happened on Soto's friends. The place they were drinking the fatal afternoon was called The Fountain of Desire (after the modest bordello in the back) and the owner, a bald family man nicknamed Chember, remembered it was the Captain himself who got it into his head that it would be amusing to fly everybody down to Tuxtla for a drink. "Well, no one else in that pack of cowards had ever in his life been up in the air," Chember said, "and they weren't about to start then. Until about sunset they managed to stall on the question of how many of them would fit into the Cessna. But by then Leo had snuck off long enough to put in a phone call, and Miguel's taxi was waiting for them at the door."

One of Chember's employees, a girl from the north, said, "Then suddenly that one they call the Journalist—Umberto I think is his name—remembered he had obligated himself to begin a novena for his wife's poor departed great-aunt. Huh! An excuse so false it shamed even *that* bunch into letting him off. His parting words were, 'Do it, Leo! Do it, and I will write it up for the paper and blazon your name across the heavens of Mexico—that is, at least the southern portion.' "

In his friends' version, of course, they tried to dissuade the Captain. "All the way out to the airfield in Miguel's taxi we pleaded with him," the Poet would recall. " 'But Leo, it will be like ink! How will you ever see your way down through the enveloping obscurity of the mountains? The field at Tuxtla has no night lights to speak of.' But Leo would not listen to *us*."

"He would not listen," they all agreed.

"And you know," the Artist would point out, "he very nearly made it. When we went to Tuxtla to retrieve what was left of him, they told us he only missed the end of the concrete by about ten meters. Absolutely *fantastic* flying. So near—"

"And yet," someone else would feel forced to remind the group, "so far."

"Yes," they would say, their own bleary lights beginning to wink on again, "so far."

The only remaining question, the one you heard about town for a certain time, was if Soto was really as drunk as all that, how could he even have gotten into his cockpit?

The cabdriver Miguel maintained that when it became clear the Captain would not be able to walk it, his friends carried him out across the grass to his Cessna. And then, when they had stood around stamping their feet in the gathering dusk for a while and nothing happened, Miguel said they began to get thirsty and to want to get back to town, so they went back out onto the field and put the key in Leo's ignition for him.

ROSA MARIA YBARRA

Dueños de la Tierra

Cajas de tomates
Sacos de algodón
baldes de chícharos
      manos — dark and grey
      las "forties" picked
      forty boxes al día
      championas
long sleeve shirts
cacoon gente
pick and pack and stack
      Faces dark and grey
      red and wet
      pinched and singed
      pick and pack and stack
The soil hace watch
hugging zapatos — brown and black
tired and torn
itching   sweaty faces
pick and pack and stack
      Los taquitos wrapped
      in waxed paper
      . . . que hiciera por uno
      right now
La agua
precious as gold
delicious and cold
que hiciera for a drink right now

Los "two-by-two's" esas que
trabajaban together
pick and pack and stack
faster faster
el sol calienta

Cajas de tomate
sacos de algodón
baldes de chícharos

Bus loads de Mexicanos
followed by outhouses

Bud Antle gente
tu sueño
comparto

Black Piano

My seed is a black piano
It will melt strings and smother winds
And it will burn the notes on wooden sheets
in its belly.

Chalk against its outer layer
It will erase me;
It will not call me home.
It will hold tomorrow between its teeth.
I will taste the black keys;
They will choke me.

I will spit them out
To the oak,
And I will play a song,
But instead, you will hear
The moaning of broken finger bones.

GARY YOUNG

Eating Wild Mushrooms

After the rain, when the earth releases
a little wheezing breath and loosens
its brittle hold on the surface of things,

wild mushrooms appear under the trees,
against logs and along the rotting
boards behind the barn. I see them lift

the ground under the quince and spread
the scallions apart and rise, and open.
I have been shown by those who know

the slick-skinned Blewit, the Prince
like a man's head, and Satyr's Beard
with its yellow mange. But for the rest

I cultivate an ignorance and pick
puffballs a particular shade of beige,
toadstools with the prettiest cap

or purple, spongy stem. What I don't know
can't hurt me. What I do know
is that mushrooms rise from the dead

to die again, to enter the death
of whatever enters the earth. When I
pick an unfamiliar mushroom and eat it

the ground gives up for once and is cheated.
It is like kissing a stranger on the mouth.
It is knowing what you are and being forgiven.

At San Vicente Creek

The soul arrests at the soft, chalk cliffs
and holds there, like the pelicans leaning
into a senseless breeze thrown over
the water's stone channel.
Uninterrupted it shifts and penetrates the fields abutting
the ocean's mean pull. The crops, docile
and dutiful, pull it closer and expand with it. This
is satisfying. There are couples
everywhere longing for this kind
of marriage; and the wind knows, and the birds
holding themselves needlessly against their own strength
know; and the soul, which measures itself against all it caresses
knows and finds a measure for the love
it embodies but cannot possess.

BIOGRAPHICAL NOTES

FRANCISCO X. ALARCÓN, Chicano poet, editor and critic, teaches Spanish and Chicano literature and culture at the University of California at Santa Cruz. Presently, he is the president of El Centro Chicano de Escritores, a non-profit organization dedicated to the promotion of Chicano/Latino literary and artistic expressions in the greater San Francisco Bay Area.

CHARLES ATKINSON teaches writing at the University of California at Santa Cruz and has published fairly regularly in various literary magazines, including *Poetry, Virginia Quarterly Review, The Southern Review, Southwest Review* and *Poetry Northwest*.

ELLEN BASS has published several books of poetry, the most recent being *Our Stunning Harvest*. She is co-editor of *I Never Told Anyone: Writings by Women Survivors of Child Sexual Abuse* and leads workshops for survivors nationally. She is co-author (with Laura Davis) of *The Courage to Heal: A Guide for Survivors of Child Sexual Abuse*, forthcoming in spring of 1988.

BARBARA BLOOM teaches creative writing for the Santa Cruz Adult School and English at Cabrillo College. She has published one book of poems, *The Myths Do Not Tell Us*, and has another manuscript in progress. Her work has been published in various small magazines.

CLAIRE BRAZ-VALENTINE is a free-lance writer, poet, and playwright. She has had five plays produced, and lives in Santa Cruz with her Boston terrier, Clancy.

WILFREDO Q. CASTAÑO is the author of *Small Stones Cast Upon the Tender Earth*. He won first place in Poetry in the UC Irvine Literary Awards in 1983. He is on the faculty at San Francisco City College and has an M.A. from San Francisco State University.

LUCILLE CLIFTON is the author of six books of poetry. Her latest books are *Good Woman* (collected poems and a memoir) and *Next* (new poems). Both books will be published in the fall of 1987. *Two-Headed Woman* won the Juniper Prize and was nominated for the Pulitzer. She teaches at the University of California at Santa Cruz. She has read her poems across the country and is former Poet Laureate of Maryland.

FLORINDA COLAVIN has been published in *Ariadne's Thread, In Celebration of the Muse, Ally* and she's read in several of the "In Celebration of the Muse" readings. She has also led journal workshops.

JOSEPH DRUCKER is editor of *Ally*, a poetry journal. His latest collection is *A Brother Remembered*. His work has been published in several journals including *New York Poets Cooperative, Bay Area Poets Coalition Anthology* and *Blue Unicorn*.

WILLIAM EVERSON, also known as Brother Antoninus, turned 75 in September, 1987. *New Directions* is publishing his biography in 1988. Stanford University Press brought out his book on Robinson Jeffers in fall 1987. Everson has written over 30 books of poetry and criticism.

GEORGE FULLER is a freelance writer. He served as editor of *Monterey Life*, and is editor and publisher of the chapbook series, *Poet Santa Cruz* and Jazz Press. His publications include *Adam and Eve*.

JAMES B. HALL is a novelist, short story writer, and poet who currently resides in Santa Cruz. His work is widely anthologized.

GEORGE HITCHCOCK has lived in Santa Cruz for the past 18 years. He teaches at the University of California at Santa Cruz.

JAMES D. HOUSTON is the author of five novels, including *Love Life* (1985) and *Continental Drift* (1978), both from Alfred Knopf. "The Dangerous Uncle" comes from his most recent non-fiction work, *The Men in My Life*.

JEANNE WAKATSUKI HOUSTON co-authored *Farewell to Manzanar*, the story of her family's World War Two experience. She also co-wrote the teleplay, based on this book, which became an NBC World Premiere Movie. The excerpt printed here is from her first novel, *Chiba and the Fire Horse Woman*.

BARBARA HULL teaches creative writing and literature at San Jose State University. Her work has been published in *California Quarterly, Poetry, Seattle Review* and others.

PAULA JONES teaches writing at Cabrillo College and spends summers in the Sierras. She's read locally in the "In Celebration of the Muse" series and on KUSP-FM, and had poetry published in *Matrix*.

STEPHEN KESSLER is editor and publisher of *The Sun*. His two books of poetry are *Nostalgia of Fortune Teller* and *Living Expenses*. His translations include *Widows*, a novel by Ariel Dorfman, and *Changing Centuries*, selected poems of Fernando Alegría.

EDWARD KING-SMYTH studies at the American College of Traditional Chinese Medicine. He has published in the book review section of the *San Francisco Chronicle*, in *Pacific Discovery*, and in the University of California at Santa Cruz literary magazine, *Chinquapin*.

ROSIE KING-SMYTH holds a Ph.D. from the University of California at Santa Cruz with a dissertation on the poetry of H.D. Her poems have appeared in *Dark Horse*, *California Quarterly* and *San Jose Studies*.

ROBERT LUNDQUIST, a resident of Santa Cruz, California, hopes some day to be a resident of Paris, France or Camogli, Italy.

LYNN LURIA-SUKENICK has published four books of poetry, including *Houdini Houdini*. Her fiction has appeared in several journals and her criticism has been published in *The Village Voice, Ironwood, The American Book Review* and others. She has taught at Cornell University, the University of California and the University of Arizona. She is currently a consultant in writing and writing/healing in Santa Cruz.

ROBERT MCDOWELL is the author of *Quiet Money*. With Mark Jarman, he co-edits *The Reaper* and Story Line Press.

JOAN MCMILLAN lives in Corralitos with her husband and three children. Her poetry has appeared in local publications including *The Porter Gulch Review* and *In Celebration of the Muse*. Joan teaches poetry workshops in Santa Cruz schools through the Spectra Arts Program.

DUNCAN MCNAUGHTON, born in Boston in 1942, has been living in and out of Santa Cruz since 1980. His books include *Dream* (1972),

A Passage of Saint Devil (1976), *Sumeriana* (1977), *Shit on My Shoes* (1979) and *Sonny Boy* (1983).

NATHANIEL MACKEY is the author of *Four for Trane*, Golemics (1978); *Septet for the End of Time*, Boneset (1983); *Eroding Witness*, University of Illinois Press (1985). He also wrote *Bedouin Hornbook*, Callaloo Fiction Series (1986). He is the editor and publisher of *Hambone*.

TOM MADEROS, author of the manuscript *American Nights*, lived in New York, Paris and Mallorca. He turned down acceptance to grad school at Yale (graphic design) for fear of a withering career designing Ex Lax ads.

MORTON MARCUS is author of seven books (including *Origins, The Santa Cruz Mountain Poems* and *Big Winds, Glass Mornings, Shadows Cast By Stars*). He has had poems in more than 100 magazines and 50 anthologies. His sixth book of poems, *Pages from a Scrapbook of Immigrants*, will be published by Coffee House Press in 1988. He is co-host of the KUSP-FM poetry show.

STEPHEN MEADOWS, a native Californian of American Indian descent, has studied with the poets William Everson, Lucille Clifton and the late Kenneth Rexroth. His poems have appeared nationwide, most notably in *The Laurel Review* and *The Clouds Threw This Light*, a definitive anthology of native American poetry. He donates much of his time to public radio and political causes.

MAUDE MEEHAN, author of *Chipping Bone*, is a writer, wife, mother, editor, lecturer, and political activist. For several years she has been leading creative writing workshops for women in Santa Cruz.

HARRYETTE MULLEN has published *Tree Tall Woman*, Energy Earth (1982); she has appeared in the following anthologies: *Her Work*, Schearer Publication Company (1982); *South by Southwest*, University of Texas Press (1986); *Washing the Cows' Skulls*, Prickly Pear Press (1982). She is from Texas.

SHARMAN MURPHY has lived in the Santa Cruz area off and on since 1969. She teaches for the California Poets in the Schools program.

TILLIE OLSEN's works include: *Tell Me a Riddle, Silences, Yonnondio* and *Mother to Daughter/Daughter to Mother*. She has received a Guggenheim Fellowship, and won the O'Henry Award for the best short story of 1961. Her daughter, Julie Olsen Edwards, teaches at Cabrillo College, Santa Cruz, in Early Childhood Education.

SHERRI PARIS has been writing fiction and poetry for ten years. She writes for *The Sun* and teaches writing at the University of California at Santa Cruz.

DALE PENDELL was the founding editor of *Kuksu*. He is widely published in literary magazines and has a book entitled *Physics for the Heart*.

VICTOR PERERA publishes widely as a freelance journalist. He is the author of the books: *The Conversion, The Last Lords of Palenque* and *Rites*. *Rites* won the Present Tense Award for biography.

ROBERT PETERSON has published eight books of poetry, including *Waiting for Garbo*, Black Dog Press (1987). He received a National Endowment for the Arts grant in 1967 and an Amy Lowell Traveling Fellowship in 1972. He grew up in San Francisco and served in World War II as a medic.

BERNICE RENDRICK lives and writes in Scotts Valley. She has new poetry coming out in *Kansas Quarterly* and *Quarry West*. She has work included in the anthology, *In Celebration of the Muse*.

ADRIENNE RICH is the author of many books of poetry and essays, the most recent of which are *Blood, Bread and Poetry* (1985) and *Your Native Land, Your Life: Poems* (1986). She is active in New Jewish Agenda.

GAËL ROZIÈRE, raised in Mexico, France and the United States, is the author of *Witness to a Landscape* and *Somos Tres*. She co-founded the series "In Celebration of the Muse" and for fourteen years has lived in Santa Cruz where she writes and takes care of her two children.

PRISCILLA (TILLY) W. SHAW is originally from New England, teaches at the University of California at Santa Cruz, and has been writing poetry for a few years.

TIMOTHY SHEEHAN is the author of *Here*, Brandenburg Press; *Yes*, Green House Review Press, and was anthologized in *Songs from an Unsung World*, Science '85. Timothy is a licensed sail plane pilot.

MARJORIE SIMON's poems appear in *Adam and Eve etc.* and in *The Long Distance Oatmeal Eater*.

PHILLIP SLATER, author of *How I Saved the World*, left a university career in 1971 to write. His previous books include *Pursuit of Loneliness* and *Wealth Addiction*. Slater is currently working on a second novel.

ROZ SPAFFORD teaches writing at the University of California at Santa Cruz, participating in the Women's Re-Entry Program and writes a column of political commentary and cultural criticism for *The Sun*, a Santa Cruz weekly. She is also a negotiator for her union, the American Federation of Teachers. Since 1980, her poetry and fiction have centered on issues relating to nuclear war.

CAROL STAUDACHER is an author in the field of mental health, a poet, and an editor. Her poetry has appeared in numerous literary journals and anthologies including the *New York Quarterly*, *Five Fingers Review*, *Primavera*, and *In Celebration of the Muse*. Her most recent non-fiction books are *Hypnosis for Change* (1985) and *Beyond Grief* (1987).

JOSEPH STROUD's first book, *In the Sleep of Rivers*, was published by Capra Press. *Signatures*, his second book, was published by BOA Editions. He appeared in the anthology *19 New American Poets of the Golden Gate*, Harcourt, Brace, Jovanovich. He teaches at Cabrillo College and is co-host of the KUSP-FM poetry show.

JAN STURTEVANT began writing seriously in 1983; she writes poetry as well as prose and has been the poetry editor for the Mr. Toots newsletter since 1985. Dedicated to the journal process, she teaches Room to Write journal workshops for women.

AMBER COVERDALE SUMRALL is co-director of the Santa Cruz women writers reading series, "In Celebration of the Muse." She is co-editor of *In Celebration of the Muse: Writings by Santa Cruz Women* and *Touching Fire: Erotic Writing by Women* (forthcoming). Her work appears in *Passages North, The Greenfield Review, Ikon, Porter Gulch Review, Sinister Wisdom,* and *With the Power of Each Breath.*

DAVID SWANGER is the author of three books: *The Poem as Process,* and two books of poetry, *The Shape of Waters* and *Inside the Norse.* He lives, works, and writes in Santa Cruz.

ROBERT SWARD, author of *Poet Santa Cruz* (Jazz Press) and twelve other books of poetry, teaches at Monterey Peninsula College. Currently, he co-coordinates the Santa Cruz reading series for Local 7 of the National Writers' Union.

MARK TAYLOR lives in the Santa Cruz mountains and is writing screenplays.

LOUISE THORNTON teaches writing at Cabrillo and Gavilan Colleges. She co-edited with Ellen Bass *I Never Told Anyone: Writings by Women Survivors of Child Sexual Abuse.* She's currently working on an anthology of women's erotica with Jan Sturtevant and Amber Coverdale Sumrall.

PATRICE VECCHIONE is co-editor of *In Celebration of the Muse: Writings by Santa Cruz Women* and co-director of the Muse reading series. Her work has been published in several journals and anthologies. She coordinates the California Poets in the Schools program for Santa Cruz and San Benito Counties.

ALMA LUZ VILLANUEVA is the author of *Blood Riot, Mother May I, La Chingada,* and *Life Spans,* a collection of poetry. She is also the author of a novel, *The Ultra Violet Sky,* to be published in 1987. She has an MFA in Creative Writing from Goddard College. She is at work on her second novel and another book of poetry.

T. MIKE WALKER teaches writing at Cabrillo College. His novel *Voices from the Bottom of the World: a Policeman's Journal* was published by Grove Press. The piece published here is excerpted from *The Last American,* a novel in progress.

SARA WALSH has been published in the *Porter Gulch Review, The Good Times, Survival Shuffle Press,* and *Shambhala Press.* She is a soccer player, a bookbinder, and a member of the Artisans' Cooperative in Santa Cruz.

KEN WEISNER is the editor of *Quarry West*. Summer 1987 *Antioch Review* published four of his poems. He has also published in *Pocket Pal*, *New Honolulu Review* and *Eye Prayer*. His translation of work by contemporary Peruvian poet, Carlos Belli, appeared in *Seneca Review*.

STEVE WIESINGER has appeared in *IMAGE*, *An Asia Notebook*, *Monterey Life*, and other magazines and anthologies. He received a James D. Phelan award, and a California Arts Council grant while teaching in the state prisons. He co-edited the prison anthology, *About Time II*.

ANITA WILKINS' two books, *Talking to the Blindman* and *The Trees Along This Road*, are published with Blackwells Press. She teaches writing at Cabrillo College.

KIRBY WILKINS is the author of *Vanishing*, a book of short stories, and *King Season*, a novel. He teaches writing at Cabrillo College.

CARTER WILSON's novels, *Crazy February* and *A Green Tree and a Day Tree* are set in Mayan villages in Mexico, where Wilson worked as an anthropologist in the 1960s. Another, *Treasures on Earth*, takes place in the Peruvian Andes. With Judith Coburn, Wilson wrote the narration for the Oscar-winning documentary, "The Life and Times of Harvey Milk."

ROSA MARIA YBARRA focuses on her heritage: the Chicana experience. Viewing her craft as a form of creative protest, Ybarra examines society's stereotypes of Chicanos and Mexicanos.

GARY YOUNG is an award winning poet and artist whose honors include grants from the National Endowment for the Arts, the National Endowment for the Humanities, and the James D. Phelan Literary Award. His latest book is *In the Durable World*. He is editor of Greenhouse Review Press.